O9-BTI-915

TRICK OF THE EYE

TRICK OF THE EYE

Dennis Haseley

Dial Books • New York

Published by Dial Books
A member of Penguin Group (USA) Inc.
345 Hudson Street
New York, New York 10014

Designed by Nancy R. Leo-Kelly
Text set in Dante
Printed in the U.S.A. on acid-free paper
1 3 5 7 9 10 8 6 4 2

Library of Congress Cataloging-in-Publication Data
Haseley, Dennis.
Trick of the eye / Dennis Haseley.
p. cm.
Summary: Upon discovering that he can enter paintings and speak with the people in them, a twelve-year-old boy sets out on a journey of discovery that ultimately leads to his own forgotten past.
ISBN 0-8037-2856-5
[1. Emotional problems—Fiction. 2. Art—Fiction. 3. Memory—Fiction. 4. Mothers and sons—Fiction. 5. Painters—Fiction. 6. England—Fiction.] I. Title.
PZ7.H2688Tr 2004 [Fic]—dc22 2003010400

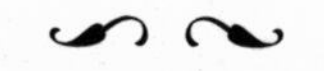

TRICK OF THE EYE

Chapter 1

As a clue to a crime it seemed so very little; but as would become clear, that was because the real offense was not mentioned, and the only witness locked away.

The boy saw the story on the Friday after the incident, came upon it clipped out of a newspaper where his mother had laid it, on a side table outside the room where she worked. As if she had forgotten it, she had put her pocketbook on top of it—it took sharp eyes to see the clipping at all.

It was considered a humorous mystery. On a Wednesday morning, the owner of a gallery unlocked the front door, and immediately upon entering, saw it: some sort of monkey, in a small blue coat. It was sitting on the floor, near where it had "done its business"—as the owner's niece later said—and it was gazing up at a painting done in the Impressionist style. It was not a painting attributed to any of the Frenchmen who had gained notoriety on the Continent, but that of an almost unknown artist, whose work the owner of the gallery had taken a fancy to. The painting itself showed a lovely young woman, dressed in blue, with a large hat, seated on a swing, and looking out directly at the viewer—in this case, the monkey—with the fluidity of color, the lack of definition, and the illusion of moving light that such paintings were known for. There was nothing remarkable about the work.

No one was quite sure how the animal had entered. A recently-hired assistant protested that he had indeed locked the door, and inquiries at zoos and circuses did not trace the beast. What made the scene more unusual was the fact that the animal, while cocking its head as it stared at the portrait, was lifting its arm—holding it there—and then slowly dropping it. Almost as if the animal were making an exaggerated mimicry of using a brush.

And then came the punch line: The monkey could probably do a better job of it.

"It doesn't say he hurt anything," the boy said aloud, although there was no one there, not even a painting on the wall of the room where he stood. He tried to picture what the gallery looked like, the landscapes and portraits extending along the walls of it, and the beast perhaps lost in this hall of art. He wondered how the monkey had entered, and what had become of it. He was going to put the clipping back beneath the purse, when his eye was again caught by the phrase about the monkey's arm, rising and falling, and the way it had stared at the woman in blue, in the hat, on the swing. How the beast must have looked at her face, perhaps waiting for a response, not understanding that it had been tricked.

With the fragment of paper still in his hand, the boy walked through the house, and listened at the back door. He could hear the hollow clicking sound his mother made as she worked in her garden, cutting the weeds, thinning the leaves from the roses; he could just see the bottoms of her Wellingtons sticking out from the hedge, and inching slightly forward as she progressed.

Upstairs in his room, he put the article on his bed, and he read it again. He wondered why his mother would cut it out; she was a writer on etiquette, a newspaper expert on manners, and an animal befouling a cultivated room would be the last thing she was interested in, unless by way of example. He turned the piece of newsprint over. On the other side was a letter to the editor complaining of how people never cover their mouths and say "Excuse me" when they cough on the trains. Perhaps that would be why she cut it out—although she'd done an uneven job of it: Part of the letter was missing.

He turned the clipping around; he wanted to read it again before returning it. For he suddenly had his own idea about how the monkey had gotten in.

He looked up from where he sat on his bed, gazed at the things from long ago: the stuffed dragon his mother had once given him, a lion with an almost human face, the little figure of the gray-bearded sailor she said his father had sent him. Even though his mother was downstairs, and his father was long ago gone, these things seemed filled with his parents' presence, as if the two of them were in the room with him. As he looked at the figures now, where they stood on his table or were spread like forms on canvas over the white coverlet of his bed, they seemed quite real, and the boy had a moment again when he understood where the monkey had come from, how it had gotten inside the gallery.

It must have stepped out of one of the paintings.

Chapter 2

The boy was standing in front of a picture of a woman—it was a woman in a hat, on a swing, dressed in blue. But now she was real, she was moving, her face gliding toward him and away. And now she was a picture again. And the boy was painting her face, moving his arm up, and then down, up and down, and he was laughing and the face of the woman was laughing and then she was still.

The boy woke with a start and the first thing he saw was the little figure of the sailor, propped on his side table with its one eyebrow lifted in a quizzical expression.

As he swung his feet to the floor, he tried to put the dream out of his mind. In a familiar routine he took the several steps to the washbasin and then stood looking in the mirror. But today even something about this struck him. When he had left the school, he'd been barely tall enough to see into the mirror, but now his face—beaded with water—was in the middle of it. He hadn't thought of the school for a long time; he was getting better and better at forgetting it. He stared at his face, keeping it very still but for the dripping water. Then he began to dry it.

He finished dressing, and walked down the stairs. Her pocketbook still sat on the small table outside the room where she worked, but the clipping, where he had returned it, was gone. If he wanted to read it again, he'd simply lost his chance.

He walked down the hall, past the frames on the wall, and for a change he let his glance linger on them. They weren't paintings; it occurred to him that his mother really didn't seem to like paintings. She had instead hung flowers, doilies, bits of oriental-looking fabric framed and pressed behind glass. There was only one proper painting in the house, in the dining room, and the dining room was where he was headed. He had started so many days like this, sleeping late, coming down for his breakfast while his mother busied herself with her work or with the garden, and eating his roll while he looked up at the colored canvas of the farm.

Sometimes he would spend quite a while sitting there, looking up at its buildings and fields and figures. Other times there might be entertainments with her. They would play cards—Beggar Your Neighbor, or War, or Old Maid. Alone, he might play Patience or Forty Thieves, and sometimes she would come in and find him and do tricks for him, the ace in her hand disappearing and showing up in his hair, in his cup, on the mantel. He would laugh, and she would after a moment laugh with him. Sometimes she would tell him stories, often about etiquette and manners, about the history of manners. He would hang on her every word.

Children used to be invited in. He remembered playing Hunt the Fox, he remembered Advancing Statues and Twenty Questions. But a table had been knocked, glass had shattered—more than once, he thought. There had been tears and running footsteps, and after a while the children hadn't come by again. He hadn't really minded, for there were once more the times with her.

That was all after they had moved here. Nine years ago they had moved here.

Before him now, the tea was still warm in its pot. He let his eyes wander over the painting; usually it gave him a great sense of peace to linger on the fields, the outbuildings and farmhouses; to see the small figures of the farmhands in the fields and the woman in the window of the house, the horse grazing by the stream.

He listened for the sound of his mother speaking to herself as she did sometimes when she wrote, for the scratching of her pen. She must be outside . . .

He had the feeling that something was wrong . . .

He glanced into the painting again, and let his gaze hold there, as an old, familiar feeling came over him, as he stared at the graceful fields. It was a sense he'd often had, when he stared into the deep colors of the canvas, or the sketched lines of a drawing in a book; yet this morning, this odd kind of longing felt stronger. How much time he gazed at the painting he didn't know.

He heard a tap that startled him from his reverie so that his cup—which he hadn't been aware of holding—half-slipped from his hand and struck his saucer. He looked up in surprise, and saw a figure—a man—standing inside his doorway, looking at him, a briefcase bulging with books under his arm. It was his tutor, of course. But what must have surprised him was the way the man extended in all directions, in three dimensions—the boy had been so lost in the painting.

~

"Master Richard."

"Mr. Roskins."

They always began this way, sitting across from each other at an empty square table in the parlor, the books in the briefcase at Roskins's feet, sometimes one open between them. The boy was reading about the history of Rome, and as Roskins asked him questions about Constantius, the emperor they were studying currently, the boy hardly looked at his tutor, but instead imagined the various scenes played out before them on the dark wooden table: senators rising to their feet to argue their points, the emperor with the crown of laurel leaves being placed on his head, the Coliseum rising in the background, and all outside the bounds of this, in the corners of the room, he could imagine the barbarians—the Franks and the Goths—hiding behind cut flowers, forming their ragged armies beneath the pillows of the sofa. Whether Roskins saw these same things in his mind's eye the boy never knew; in fact, he didn't give Roskins—a pallid man with salt-and-pepper hair, and a sour smell under his cologne—much thought, other than when he glanced up from the imaginary theater playing out between them to see his wan questioning face, with its one twitching eye.

After he'd satisfactorily answered Roskins's questions, and received the new pages to read for their next session, he accompanied Roskins to the door. He always stood there a moment, looking out through the panes of glass as Roskins walked up the gravel path toward their front gate and fence, as he stepped and grew smaller up the narrowing lines of the walk.

He turned from the door, listening for his mother. She must still be out back. He moved from the armchair to the sofa, from the parlor table to the banister of the stairs, and now back to the dining room.

He went and sat at the table, at his cleared place. The table was empty around him, an expanse of white cloth, with little wrinkles and folds, that he thought of like the lands and oceans outside Rome.

Once again he looked up at the painting.

He had that peculiar feeling again. There were the same brush-stroked little figures, the barn, the fence, the fields going away. He stood up and walked around the table, then, after pausing a moment, toward the painting. As the distance between him and the canvas narrowed, everything within the frame became wavy all at once, as if he were underwater, or as if the painting had become an Impressionist work. Now the room felt suddenly cool and there were smells of . . . grass and hay.

He had the strangest sensation that he was standing in a field of the farm.

Yes, he was standing in a field, with the other figures and buildings and the soft rise and fall of the land arrayed around. He stared at the farmhands, at the woman in the window, at the horse grazing among tall grasses that were blowing slightly in the wind. Except that they weren't blowing. Everything was absolutely still: the grass, the horse, the figures in their postures of walking or working, the light streaming over the buildings. And he was there, with the green and yellow grasses, and the short dark brown hair and darker mane of the horse, the plow with a sliver of light on its blade as it leaned against the wall of a shed, in these surroundings that somehow seemed familiar from more than the years he had gazed up at them from the table.

His sight line slowly traveled backward, and through a wooden square that must be the frame, he saw the dining room, the tall windows with vanilla-colored curtains, the tablecloth with its little folds and a dark spot of the tea he had spilled earlier. He was no longer there. With absolute calm he turned his head back, and saw that the light coming over the roofs of the buildings illuminated the cloth of his shirt, as if he, now, were part of this still scene.

It all seemed right, as if he had been expecting this for so long and it had finally come to pass. Then he heard the voice.

We've been here all this time. It seemed to be coming from the woman in the window of the house.

You have? he answered. His own voice sounded somewhat dreamy, like a voice that's half-asleep in the afternoon. *But who?*

All of us. Since you were little.

He looked up at her. The window where she appeared was in the distance, and she was little more than a smear of paint, the merest suggestion of a woman. He wondered if he could somehow see fully what she would look like.

You're the same as I've always seen you, he said. *But different now, so different. I'm here. Have I been . . .* here *. . . before?*

Yes, here. And other places. Her head remained absolutely still, as did the other figures, the grass, the horse.

And I'm back now?

If you want.

Oh, I do, he said, with such emotion it surprised him.

You can always change your mind, she said.

Now, why would I?

You'd have your reasons, she said, and it seemed a sad tone had entered her voice.

Reasons? he asked.

Like what's going on here, she said. *Something anyone might want to stay away from.*

What's . . . going on? he ventured.

You can't hear it? she said.

He glanced around him at the figures in the fields, the outbuildings, the little horse. *No,* he said.

You might be able to, she said. *If you want.*

Oh, I would want to, he said, with that same charge of emotion.

You'd better go now. She's coming.

My mother?

Perhaps.

But shouldn't she know what's going on? he asked.

She knows already.

Oh, that's good. Then I can visit again?

Yes, she said. *Us. And others.*

Others?

You'll find out. If you want. You'd best hurry now.

He stood shakily on the floor with his hand outstretched as he heard his mother approach the room.

Chapter 3

When his mother entered, he was once again sitting at the dining room table in his chair. The tablecloth still stretched around him, white, with its little folds. It could look as if he'd never even left his seat, as if he'd been staring into the painting and imagining all that had happened.

She wasn't smiling; she appeared preoccupied. She wouldn't be running her hand over his hair as she came close, asking him how his tea had been. She took off the gloves she was wearing. The boy watched her slowly lay them down on a table by the back door, as if they were hands with the life going out of them. She came over to the table, shaking her head, and stood by him.

"They're spoiling the roses," she said.

"Who is?" He didn't look up.

"It's almost a pretty name. 'Aphid.' Like a kind of angel or sprite. But it disguises the terrible things they're doing to the roses."

"What are they doing?"

"Eating away their life," she said, and walked away.

His shoulders sank. He hadn't seen her in one of her dark moods in quite a while, and in the interval he had begun to believe they would not return again. Where they came from, and what caused them to finally fade, seemed as mysterious as the formation and dispersal of clouds. And seeing the set look on her face, he feared that this one might prove worse than most, heavy weather that might move in and stay.

He glanced up at the painting. It was like a garden of roses—so wonderful to look at—but there were things wrong there, as well. Perhaps there was something he could do to help them with whatever the trouble was, help them in their still and quiet world.

And maybe, for a longer time, he'd be able to stay.

In the drawing room his mother sat at a large table of dark walnut, before a squared stack of oversized paper called foolscap, a pot of dipping ink, and her pens, lined up one, two, three. He stood just outside the doorway, listening to the crisp slitting sound she made with her letter opener as she attended to a small stack of envelopes. She didn't see him, and yet he could see her. He could listen to the crackling of the paper as she opened the letters, the almost imperceptible sound as she laid them before her, and then the scratching of the pen on the foolscap as she answered the letters from her readers, instructing wives what to do about husbands who were remiss in removing their hats, who wiped their hands on the tablecloth, or suggesting to beleaguered parents the order of the relatives that needed to be informed on the breaking of an engagement.

History itself was a kind of teacher of manners, she maintained; it told you how conventions had developed, and why they became established. For instance, in an untamed world, a guest stepping over the threshold of a host could seem a threat—and so over the years they became bound by hospitality. The word *etiquette* itself was related to the word *ticket*—a label or sticker that told what something was, where its rightful place should be. As she had taught him, so he knew these and other odd bits of things, such as the history of the term *foolscap*: that it referred to the seal or watermark in the form of a jester's hat that appeared on the paper she used.

Yet with all this he didn't know what he was feeling as he made his way back to the dining room; nor did he understand the wave of longing inside him as once more he stood, his back to the dining room table, and looked into the picture of the farm.

He stared across the fields, at the face of the woman in the window. She didn't move, nor say anything, and once again he felt his shoulders slump.

Then, after a moment, he heard low voices: A man, standing before him as near as across the table, was speaking to a figure in the field—a burly boy in coveralls.

It's terrible. What shall we do?

I think I'll go mad, said the burly boy.

By concentrating, he could hear them quite distinctly. He realized he was once more in the field with them.

What's terrible? he finally asked.

Who's there? It was the stable man who answered.

It's I, said the boy. *Richard.* It felt odd to say his name to strangers.

Glory be! exclaimed the man, and then said no more. It seemed as if what life he'd had had gone out of him, and the boy worried that without meaning to, he had somehow crushed this figure of paint and line, like a fragile toy.

Now, don't you try anything! cried the burly boy.

I'm not going to try anything, said Richard.

You're one of them, ain't ya?

One of whom—and what's happened to him, and what's so terrible? He glanced to the window, but imagined the woman looking out now with unseeing eyes.

I expect he's gone faint, said the young man. *Erin, Erin,* he called, which seemed to have an effect, as the stable man came back to life.

He faints? Standing up?

Of course he does. But I shouldn't be talkin' to ya—he's one of them, all right, Erin.

The boy of course did appear quite different from the figures he was talking to. His body looked solid, but theirs were composed of brushstrokes; their hands weren't entirely formed, and their faces—on closer examination—were merely suggestions of faces.

For a moment it seemed he was noticing these differences from where he stood by the table, staring into the painting.

The next instant he was with them again.

You don't need to worry about him, lads! said the woman at last. *He's here to help us. It's just that he doesn't yet know.*

Thank you, said Richard politely. *That's right, I don't know.*

Likely, said the burly boy. The others continued to stare at him in the postures they'd been in all along.

A man in the farthest reaches of the field, who was kneeling, looking at the bottom part of a fence, now called out: *You mean you can't hear it?*

Just as the man said that, a high-pitched sound, a crying of something, came to his ears.

Careful now, Martin, said Erin.

I can hear it now, said Richard. He glanced at them all, still caught up in the wonder of being there. The high-pitched crying ran through his head like a wire. *What is it?*

It's the horse.

And now that the man identified the sound, Richard could discern that it was that of painful whinnying.

He drew closer to the man who was kneeling by the fence. When he had gazed on the print from the dining room, he had always been intrigued by what the man was doing, he seemed so intent on his labor.

But why?

The man didn't change his posture.

Why don't you look at me?

Once again, the man didn't move.

The boy glanced from one to the other. *You can't,* the boy said, suddenly understanding what was obvious, but in a way he hadn't quite understood before. *You can't move—you've been painted here, and now you can't change.*

And you can, said Martin. *And that's what's frightened the horse.*

It has?

They remained in their silent and still postures.

But why? asked the boy again. *I'm not going to hurt you.* He could see how the stream wasn't moving—just the illusion of it. Whatever danger they might be feeling, he felt entirely safe. He was in a universe that couldn't move or suddenly shift, the half-world he'd often gazed upon, of puppets and toys, of bedtime animals from long ago.

He felt an upsurge of joy, and he felt like taking a step, a little leap, really, over a silver stroke that was supposed to be a rock.

He heard a gasp from the burly boy, and Erin spoke. *He's one, all right. He's a mover, Martin.*

That he is, said Martin.

The horse, which had begun to quiet, now began an even higher-pitched crying.

But I told you I'm not going to hurt anyone, said Richard.

Just hold still for a while, said the woman, *and let's see if that works.*

He did as he was told, and after a few minutes went by, the horse once again grew quiet.

The boy stood motionless by the fence. *What is it?* he whispered. Once again the same shift in perspective and distance occurred—he momentarily felt the table against his back—and then he was again in the field.

Shhhhh, said Martin.

Is it really my moving?

More's the pity of it, said the woman.

But why?

Now how are we supposed to know, him being a horse? said the burly boy.

After a pause, the woman spoke. *It's what's there,* she said. *What he saw.*

Here?

No.

How could it be somewhere else? You're all in this . . . place.

It's not in this place, said the woman.

Slowly the boy moved his head, till he gazed at the now quiet horse. The horse—more than any of them—was staring out, and would be staring out into whatever room the painting was hung.

Out there, said the woman. *That's what's scared him so.*

Richard glanced back into the room, at the empty table. Softly he said, *I don't always like it there either. You say I'm a mover, but what if I don't want to be? What if I . . . wanted to stay.*

Come now, said the burly boy.

And be with you here, said Richard.

If you want, said Martin slowly.

Martin! said the stable hand.

I do, said the boy. *Maybe I've always wanted to.*

He stayed as he was a minute. Not moving. Everything was still around him. Still.

After a little while longer he said, *What the horse saw—it wasn't in this room, was it?*

But now they in their turn were silent, and no matter what he said to them, or what movements he made, they would not speak. The only result of his question was the renewed and terrified whinnying of the horse.

Chapter 4

Later that afternoon, he heard voices coming from the little sunroom off the kitchen—women's voices, his mother's among them. He stuck his head around a corner, and saw them before he withdrew. The ladies were there, in their crisp dresses and white gloves, sitting at a table set for early tea. There was polite laughter among them; he glimpsed his mother—a tall attractive woman with deep-set eyes and brown hair threaded with gray—lifting a small sandwich from a plate, and he saw in that instant that she had not been one of those who was laughing.

As if to comfort himself, he focused on the small details he had glimpsed: the large earthenware teapot, the silver creamer and sugar bowl. The doilies that matched the lace centerpiece; the little silver spoons that had the figure of cupid engraved on their backs, which his mother sometimes set facedown . . .

Laughter rose again; it poured from the room like the sun on the white wicker table and chairs, and reminded him of the light falling on the buildings of the farm, but his mother's voice was still missing from the gaiety.

He walked down the hall. New things were starting to happen, and it gave him an unsettled feeling. It wasn't just the way she was being at tea, which he feared was a continuation of her troubled humor.

He ticked the other new things off on his fingers. A new cook had been hired—it was she who would have made the sandwiches, set out the cups and saucers. She had already passed over the threshold and he still hadn't laid eyes on her.

Lastly—he touched his third finger—there was the thing he had to do. And that was new, that was odd for him, something he *had* to do, something he *wanted* to do, other than read the lessons for Roskins, take meals with his mother and listen closely to her instruction.

The unsettled feeling remained as he climbed the stairs, and the sense of oddness made the wooden banister and red-and-yellow carpeting below his feet seem momentarily to be the stairs of a different house. He climbed the steps and entered his room, which was cluttered with his books and old toys—the wind-up locomotive and track, the whirligigs he and his mother in happy times had launched over the stove, and the figures, of course, from her and his father—and it was odd how he knew almost perfectly where to find the set of paints, the little tin of watercolors, which he'd forgotten he had, that was on the bottom of a box on his second shelf and was wrapped around with a bit of frayed blue ribbon.

The box clicked open, and he didn't understand why he started at the sound, why he felt the need to go to his door and listen for the buzz of conversation of the tea, to locate his mother in that room while he was here in his. The little squares of paint were dry and cracked, the brush had turned into a stick. But he wondered now, and that was also something he rarely did. He wondered if you put a little water onto the paints, if you couldn't make them wet again, and ready to flow.

He's back, Martin, said the burly boy.

That I am, said Richard, trying to echo the style of their speech.

And he's got something, something in his hand, Erin chimed in.

What is it? asked the woman in the window, and Richard slowly—so as not to frighten the horse—held it up.

A little box, said the burly boy.

It's only paints, he said, and the woman cried out, *Oh, He is the Creator, oh, Sir, we are sorry if we have offended Thee.*

Sorry, sorry, sorry, said a chorus of whispering voices, a sound like a breeze. It seemed to be coming from the grass at his feet.

Who's the Creator? asked Richard.

He isn't then, said the burly boy.

I don't know, said Richard.

Then why do you have the watercolors? asked Martin.

How can you tell they're watercolors, asked Richard, *if you're turned around?*

But the figures stayed silent.

Why do you have them? Martin inquired again.

Would you paint us out? asked Erin suddenly. *He could,* he said to the others, *if he were the Creator. He could give, or he could paint over, cover us over.*

The horse started whinnying again, high and incessant.

Of course I wouldn't do such a thing, said Richard, at the same time realizing he could, understanding that to them, paints were as lethal as a sword.

I wouldn't, he began again, *and neither would . . .* He understood at once, that by the Creator, they meant whoever had painted them. *And neither would the Creator,* he said.

Don't be sure, said Martin. *There were more of us, in the painting—you can't see. He painted them, and then He chose not to use them. So He painted them over.*

He could give, or He could paint over, said Erin excitedly.

It made Richard slightly dizzy, to think of someone being painted over.

Well, I *wouldn't,* he said. *I only have the paints so I can help the horse. Help his fear.*

He paused and took a breath. *I can give him blinders,* he said. *That way, he won't see us moving, when we walk past, in the room. We'd never given it a thought, you see, and now it'll be taken care of. Of course, only if he wants,* he added quickly.

He might like that, said Erin.

How will you do it? asked the woman, almost at the same time.

I could paint *them on.* There was a hush over them again, as if they were frightened at the enormity of what he'd said, of the force contained in his tin of colors and brush.

You don't have to worry, he added, almost fiercely. *Why do you think I'm here? You think I'd do—whatever the horse saw?*

There was no response. After a moment, he walked slowly toward the horse, which sensed his approach and made a blowing sound through its nostrils. He stepped past the barn, where he could see little dabs of paint, and places where the paint hadn't adhered on the windows, and the canvas beneath showed through, that was supposed to give the illusion of hay. He stepped over rocks, and walked along the fence into the pleasant distance, and for a breathless moment he wondered about those beneath the surface, who had been there once, and then were painted over.

The animal was just ahead now, and he reached its side and halted. He could see how its head was painted straight on, foreshortened, and staring into the room—this room, or some other. He opened the tin of paints—the click made the horse snort—and he took the brush from his pocket and reached toward the animal. The other figures were hushed, the horse was trembling—no, it was his own hand that was shaking.

It's okay. It's all right, he said, speaking quietly to the horse, trying to soothe it. *Blinders,* he added, *so you won't see what's in the room.*

The black-tipped brush was almost touching the horse now, its point almost on its bridle where the leather patches would extend.

Wait, said Martin.

The boy froze his hand.

It's not going to help, said Martin. *He'll see it even if it's not there. Even if he's blinded.*

That doesn't make any sense, the boy said testily. *It'll still help.* Once again, standing on tiptoes—on what for a moment seemed the dining room floor—he brought forward the black-tipped brush.

There's something more, said the woman from the window.

More?

That maybe he's still needing to see.

Needing? asked the boy. He slowly lowered the brush. *Why would he be needing to, if it scares him so?*

There was no answer. After a moment: *You know there were others,* said Martin. *Who saw what he saw. Others there, besides the horse.*

Others? said the boy. The word had an echo for him.

One was an angel, holding a mirror.

The boy lowered his head. *I do remember an angel,* he said, *holding a mirror. I remember I used to talk to him. When I was little.*

You used to, when you were very little, said Martin.

Can I find him again? asked the boy.

Yes, said Martin.

If you want to, said Erin.

Of course I do, said the boy, looking over at Martin. His face was still turned away, as it would always be.

The horse looked more frightened than ever. *It'll be okay,* the boy said to the horse. *Perhaps if I find the others, and find what scares you so.*

Or you could stay here with us, said Martin.

Stay here with you, said the boy. *Yes, I still think of that.*

Those ones he saw—they were moving, said Martin, as the horse once again began its high-pitched cry.

Moments later he was standing at the front door of his house, where it opened onto the yard. He stared through the framed windows; he could see the large rectangle of the green lawn, the stone fence in a line, the square gate, the trees beyond with their hanging branches, all crisscrossed lines; and beyond the trees, above them, a narrow band of sky cast with clouds where the rays of the sun shifted. On certain days he had walked the perimeter of the yard, gone with his mother through rectangular doors to shops or the houses of a few of her friends; had even gone by himself to the neighboring streets to fetch ink for her, or stationery—but it was hard for him to remember much of it, whom he'd seen on the streets or what the shopkeepers said. The sun was shining down on his yard, the grass a brighter green in its light and everything still. It took a great force of imagination or will to think of the sun shining on other places, to remember those other places he'd been. When he happened to see people walk by, he thought of them as mechanical ducks on a shooting range, following their track—and where they were going to or coming from, he didn't consider. But to think of them all out there, all at once: It would be a confusion of speech and gesture, like an endless tea party of mismatched plates and spilling food. He had come here to get away from what he heard or thought he heard from the figures in the painting, but now he had the sudden worry as he looked out the window that he would go vaulting through its glass and land out there amongst the chaotic crowds of the world, into sudden movements and the sunlight flooding all around.

He took a breath. Hadn't his mother warned him that others might not know the rules? There was danger passing over either side of a threshold, for you never knew what some of them might do, you could never be too sure of those movers . . .

He put his fingers against the window glass.

They said the horse had seen something moving in a room.

He turned from the window, and the walls seemed to rise around him, as the conviction rose in him.

It wasn't this room; not that one. Not the one where his mother was having tea.

He turned again, with a sinking feeling, and the knowledge that there was another room outside of this house, through the gate, on the other side of the fence. A room where the painting had once hung, a room where there was something else in pain, waiting for him to come. He could picture it clearly: It was an angel holding a mirror.

There was movement ahead of him, and he started. A figure was walking toward the doorway where he stood, growing larger along the sight lines. He watched a further moment until it was clear that it was the slightly stooped figure of Roskins, his tutor.

Chapter 5

"Master Richard?" said Roskins.

"Yes?" answered Richard, staring across him at the table, seeing it all in a flash, his own blinders failing him.

The school had been a large brick building with lawns, but there had been jostling in the halls, and fights, one against one, and mean things said, sharp words and insults. Sometimes to escape this he would sit in class and look out through the tall windows with their wavy glass, out at the lawns, the boys from the upper grades in their whites kicking around a soccer ball, but this gave him little relief. For the way he might accidentally move his head as he watched made the grass seem to shift like a ridge of water. And sometimes he would think of the uniforms as gulls, the whole lawn as waving sea grass, and the ball as someone's head, still floating there, still floating, only needing a little longer to hold on until help came.

It was the day of the upper class theatrical that had brought these images to their climax and made it so he had to leave. He was in the auditorium, not really comfortable with the other children, but sitting with them, when the curtain jerkily opened and boys dressed as seamen walked onto the stage. Those on either side of him began to clap at some effect, and he heard sweeping through the audience the ripples of applause before his glance went back to the set. The stage itself was tilting, back and forth, up and down, but the thing that seemed to be generating the acclaim was the waves that were all around it. Not really waves, of course, but yards of fabric the young stagehands were billowing, making false ridges of water roll along the cloth. Staring at them, he had felt he was seeing now, rushing over him, what he had only been calmly told of years before. He had sprung up from his seat and flailed across the bodies in his row, as if swimming for his own life toward the aisle. Then he ran for the door, trying to wipe away that rolling vision from his eyes.

When they brought him to the headmaster, there had been a ship in a bottle on his desk, with a cork in its end. When they told him his mother had been sent for, he himself had grown oddly calm, and carefully explained to the headmaster in his child's voice that the cork should not be there, for if there were little figures on the ship, they would not get enough air. They would have the sensation of not being able to breathe. The sensation of drowning. He could still remember the headmaster tilting his head as he looked at him, as if seeing something he could not understand, while someone whispered in the man's ear.

The way his mother had told him the story, carefully and slowly, like laying out forks and knives for a formal dinner, was that they had found the spars and parts of the mast, they'd salvaged a life preserver with the name of the ship, *The Diana,* but they hadn't found any of the bodies other than the few survivors. His mother had been one of the few survivors. But his father, and the others . . .There had been a woman on the boat, dressed in blue like a sailor; there was a man with a walrus mustache who painted on deck—and they had never been seen again. And the captain had a little monkey that raced around and around. The other things she had told him, or he had imagined, he couldn't remember which; but he had pictured his parents dancing on the white ship, dancing as they passed the magical islands where there were farms and goats in fields, and lakes like mirrors. He could almost see the mustachioed man's easel tipping over, when the storm came and the ship went up and then down forever. And with a smothering feeling he sometimes imagined how the waves kept going up and up—like a cloth being pulled up—and they wouldn't stop until they covered her and covered him and covered the entire world. It was that sensation of drowning he had felt watching the theatrical. And now Roskins came twice a week . . .

"Is everything quite all right?" Roskins asked.

The boy closed his eyes a moment, then looked at his tutor and nodded. Thankfully, the images behind his eyes had faded. But even as Roskins began the day's lesson, it seemed suddenly to the boy that the very Franks and Goths they were studying were surrounding the room in which they sat, threatening this fine safe kingdom with chaos.

"Master Richard?" said Roskins again.

"I'm sorry," said the boy. "I seem to be distracted."

"Yes. Shall we get on with it then?"

"Mr. Roskins," said the boy. "It's this I was wondering. I never asked you. Before you come here, where are you?"

"Excuse me?"

The boy blushed. "If you wouldn't mind so terribly much. I mean, what other places?"

"I see," said Roskins. He rubbed his forehead with his fingers, and his twitching eye grew still, looking normal, even penetrating, for an instant. "I tutor others, you see. Other young masters and misses."

"That would be in houses like this one."

"Somewhat like."

"So, they're all in these houses," said the boy, "and, pardon me for asking . . ." He had never engaged in such a long conversation with his tutor outside their subject matter. "You go from one house to another?" A pleasing, humorous but odd image now came to his mind's eye: Roskins in his striped vest, with little wings. "Like a bee, like a Mr. Bee—"

"Well, yes, I suppose, pollinating with knowledge. Now shall we . . . ?"

The boy was picturing Roskins on his rounds, tracing a map of it in his mind, from one imagined house to another, where other boys would watch him walk down their paths.

Roskins coughed. "Now, which of the political factions did the emperor favor during the Arian controversy?"

"And—excuse me, but if something else were somewhere . . . if something else were somewhere before it got here, there would also have to be a way you could know. I mean, if you couldn't ask it."

"If you couldn't ask it?" There was a bewildered, tired look on the face of the man. "What sort of thing do you mean?"

"Like that," said the boy, and pointed his finger like a pistol across the room, to a small replica of a masted ship on a bookcase shelf.

"If it didn't know," Richard continued, "and couldn't be

asked, and you couldn't . . . remember. Even though you were sure it was somewhere else. There must be a way you could still trace this thing, find out where it was, like you would on a map." He looked at Roskins, straight into his eyes, and the tutor pulled back at something he must have seen there. But the boy had looked away himself, and was once more in his own thoughts. "Because this author, Gibbon, hadn't been there, he couldn't *remember* what had happened with the Romans, but still he knew, still he . . . traced it. And he found out. All the unforeseen consequences. And one could certainly say it helped, didn't it?"

"Of course it . . . helped." The tutor glanced to the doorway.

"Then how can one find out where something was before?" He'd finally been able to come out with it.

"Well, if you mean an object"—Roskins glanced uneasily at the ship—"one could look on labels and things."

"Of course!" said the boy. "The labels on things—like a ticket. Like etiquette! Now, why didn't I think of that?"

"That's probably what the police do, when something's missing and they want to find out where it belongs," Roskins continued.

"The police . . ." said the boy. He shook his head. "They only come when there's a crime." He remembered that the police had come to the gallery he'd read of in the clipping.

"Do I catch your drift?" asked Roskins.

"Oh, yes," said the boy. "Labels." He shook his head again, and then as if a spell had lifted, the tension that had been in his body relaxed and he sat back in his chair. "The emperor favored the Eusebian faction, and that was that."

"Yes," said Roskins. "Yes, that's entirely correct." He seemed relieved to get back to the history.

~

That same afternoon he stood outside the kitchen doorway and watched the cook eat backward.

He felt like laughing as he watched this girl with her bright eyes and black bangs that framed her pale face bringing the fork to her mouth—it was as if a puppet were doing a silly thing, all on its own. She seemed to be enjoying the food, closing her eyes once as she chewed it.

Then she ate backward again—her fork in her right hand—and he did laugh this time, then saw her look slowly over at him, not with alarm, the way he would have, but more like the movement of a cat. Blinked. Smiled a little.

"Qu'est-ce que c'est?"

He tensed, and drew farther back from the doorway, until he couldn't see the part of the wooden table and bench where she sat, but just a leg of it, and the back door that gave out to the garden. She wasn't just looking at him, not just acting funny, but was speaking to him in some other language.

When he looked again, she was once more chewing, glancing over at him, her eyes dark brown and lively, a girl not that much older than he. She held up her fork and knife and smiled—she must have understood there was something about the way she held the utensils. Still she held them out . . . There was a torn-out page of a periodical tacked to the wall behind her, some sort of golden field was pictured, with a basket of apples colored in a red that went outside the borders of the black circles drawn to depict their roundness . . .

"Voulez-vous?" she said.

Behind the apples, the fields went on and on . . .

There was a tap on the back door, on its glass, and Madeline—which his mother had told him was her name—seemed a bit startled now. She looked to him, and then walked to the door, wiping her hands on her apron.

He couldn't see the figure there, but the way Madeline stepped back made him wonder what she'd seen. He could hear the voice—it had a grating sound to it.

"Lady of the house in?"

"Pardonnez-moi?"

"I've got to talk to her."

She glanced back and looked at the boy; he had moved forward, was standing directly in the doorway.

"I've got to. Is she in?"

"Je regret, non," Madeline said, for his mother was out, after tea, making a condolence call.

"Just tell her then," the man said, and the words made a kind of clash. "Tell her that Mr. B—Mr. B is back. Just tell her that."

The bobbing head that had been visible behind the girl fell out of sight. It was very unlike him to do this, but the boy went up to Madeline's side, and with her watched the figure as he walked from the door. He strolled away with an odd kind of side to side motion, dressed in rags—a flattened hat, a ripped coat with the outer part of one sleeve missing, torn pants—and what appeared to be well-made shiny boots. This last detail appeared strange to the boy, and he dropped his head, brought his hand to his mouth, and tried once again not to laugh.

~

At dinner that night, Richard sat in his usual seat, across from the farm painting, and he kept looking up at it, the burly boy and the stable man, Martin and the woman and the horse. And one time he must have kept staring at it, as if trying to see through it to the label behind, as he thought about what Roskins had said.

"Richard?"

"Yes?" He looked up at his mother, and unbelieving at first, he saw that she was smiling.

"Mrs. Morgan, one of the ladies I had to tea, remarked on you today. She stated she thought you quite the handsome young man."

"That was very nice of her," he said, blushing, basking in the compliment, basking in his mother's renewed smile.

"I thought so. Do you like the meal?"

"Oh, yes, it's lovely."

His attention reverted back, and this is what he saw: the pale flesh of the chicken on his plate, which Madeline had so relished this afternoon; the candles burning between them; the other two places set with plate and silver as was the polite custom when only two were dining at a table for four.

"Yes," he said again, nodding to her.

"I think it's fine too," she said, and smiled, and once again his heart rose to see her back to her good self. He looked to the painting again, and then to the wall below; where it was shadowed, there was a point of light from the flame that was dancing on his glass.

"I do think you can't keep your eyes still. They wander

like gypsies. All away from where you're sitting, and whom you're sitting with."

"I'm sorry," he said, looking down for a moment, as something new occurred to him, something both so simple and so unsettling, he wanted to put it out of his mind. The relief he felt at her smile was somehow not enough; it didn't put to rest all of what he had been occupied with.

"It's just that there *was* a gypsy . . ." he said. "Well, I'm not sure he was that." He poked at the fowl before him, at the bunch of grapes—it reminded him of a still life he'd seen in a book.

"A gypsy?"

"I was with . . . the cook. She eats backward." He picked up his knife and fork and demonstrated for his mother, and she gave him a knowing look.

"It's called zigzag eating," she said. "A style now popular mainly in North America. How Madeline came to favor it, I have no idea."

"And it's wrong?" he asked.

"No, it's considered proper as well. What is wrong is to mix styles. But I wouldn't be concerned with it. It's best to stick with what you know."

"Yes," he said, "with what I know." He glanced up at the painting, shadows across the far fields. "Still," he persisted, "there was a gypsy. A hobo."

"There was?"

"I saw it. Sorry, him," he said. "I didn't make it up."

"We have had some before," she said; she didn't seem at all bothered. "It's interesting, how they find their way here—thinking we'll be generous. They have their own marks, you see. A kind of a map—that only other hoboes can read. Maybe a line in the dirt. Maybe two stones in a row, with three stones above it. I wouldn't know. It's their own etiquette, I should think."

"He asked for the lady of the house."

"Did he now."

"He had a funny walk. Oh, and nice boots."

"Did he now."

"And he said, 'Tell her Mr. B is back.' What a silly thing. Madeline said he was *fou*."

"Well, I would think he was," his mother said. She shook her head, even as her deeply set eyes searched his face. For a moment, the eyes seemed to see past him, through him, to something far away. Abruptly, she looked down, and in the stillness that followed, time seemed to stop. Then, with her eyes still lowered, and with ample food still on her plate, she placed her fork at a forty-five-degree angle on the left side of her plate, and her knife at an equivalent angle on its right. All at once he saw the error he had made, how foolish he had been: For now that they were gone, he terribly missed seeing her eyes upon him, and any sign of her smile.

Chapter 6

Much later that same evening, when the lights were extinguished, the boy stopped on the stairs he was descending, holding a lamp from his room. He stayed there awhile in its dim glow, outlined in the light. He broke from that confine, as if from a spell, and started again walking slowly down the stairs, the lamp before him. His foot had caused a creak.

He could see now as he approached the painting that the rim of light cast by the lamp fell over part of the field with the road intersecting it; it was like the far edge of an eclipse, and he wondered if Erin or the woman in the window were seeing him approach like some bold comet come to lift their world from its dark enchantment, to send the rivers flowing again and make the parched flowers bloom.

Don't be alarmed, it's I, he whispered.

Why are you carryin' a light? asked the burly boy, and Richard felt a little disappointed that this was the only impression he had made.

Oh, you startled me, called Erin, and now Richard smiled.

I'm sorry if I have, he said.

Why are you here? We don't like this—this night seeing.

The boy was standing close before the picture—careful to keep the burning oil lamp away—and talking to the little figures as if he were Gulliver. He put the light on the side table beneath the painting, and screwed up the flame.

Just don't you scare the horse again, said the burly boy.

All of you, said Richard, *shouldn't be scared. I'd like to stay and visit, I'd like . . .* He gazed into the fields where they sloped to the river. The illusion was even greater in the half-light from the lamp.

I'd like to stay. But I can't. I have to . . . find something. To do what I said I was going to do. Now, hold on . . .

He heard them cry out as he began to lift the painting from the wall: Erin and the burly boy were hissing back and forth that Martin had been wrong, that they never should have trusted him, even as their own cries again overtook their words. He felt like giving the painting an extra little shake when he heard what they were saying about him, but instead, he continued his gentle, steady motion in order to get a look at its other side.

He did understand their fear: What they had thought was safe and fixed to the wall was shifting.

When the horse began its terrified whinnying, he held the painting still until the cries and voices ceased.

Martin, he said, *tell them not to be afraid.*

He brought the lantern toward the painting, and for a brief moment in its flickering light, the figures did seem to shift, to move—to be alive, really, in the way that he was alive. He thought how careful he had to be, not to set their barn or fields on fire. He crouched, brought the lantern near the wall so that its light shone onto the back of the painting. He dropped his head down and looked up.

Then he saw it, there. Faint writing on a label: *Farm Life.* Something else scratched out. And the words *Battersea Gallery, 10 Hodge Lane.*

He ducked and lifted his head out, and knelt before the scene, still holding the lantern behind it. There was an odd effect for a moment: the light shining through, the figures illuminated from the back like colored cutouts, and the barn, the fence, the horse . . .

And another patch that was thicker with paint, where the light couldn't penetrate. He leaned toward the canvas and lifted the lantern closer on its other side, careful again it wouldn't begin to burn.

He saw two faces. Indistinct, not fully formed. Simple faces, smiling—like a child might draw.

These were the ones they had told him about. The ones the Creator had covered over.

He brought the lantern away, let the painting down slowly with his other hand, and the hidden figures faded and disappeared within the charming scene of the farm.

I've got it, he said to the figures that were visible. *I mean, I know where you're from. And I'll find it. I'll ask Roskins. I'll tell him I'll need to read a map. Like the hoboes do*. He paused.

And your name. Do you want to hear your name?

But they stayed as they were, without moving, seeming suddenly lifeless: the man in the stable hand's uniform and the boy in the field, the woman daubed in the window and the man at the top of the painting, kneeling with his face turned away. He wished the man was not turned away.

I'll ask Roskins, he said again, but his words seemed to echo in the empty room. He looked from the figures in the painting to the square of the window, with its curtains drawn back, framing the blackness beyond.

But black, as he was coming to realize, could be penetrated;

it could be illuminated. Perhaps he only needed to find the proper light and hold it up, and before him would extend a shining corridor of images, a gallery beckoning him to enter.

Chapter 7

As he looked out the glass in the door, waiting for Roskins's next visit, the word *battersea, battersea* pounded in his mind like a dark ocean against a seawall. Like waves against the hull of a ship, when the sea had taken his father, and had almost taken her as well. But now, every time he began to think of that, all he saw in his mind's eye was the theatrical at school, the rolling ocean portrayed by the billowing sheets of cloth. And why should he feel so sad and scared when she'd been saved, and she was there with him? He blinked and knew that tears were drops of salt water.

Now with relief he spied Roskins approaching.

They sat as they usually did in the parlor with the pressed flowers on the wall. Two days ago he had asked Roskins for a new area of instruction, and the boy waited now to see if the man would respond. Instead of the thick book of the *Decline and Fall,* his tutor took from his briefcase a folder he laid between them.

"Maps," said Roskins.

"Oh," said the boy, "thank you so much. You remembered."

"I must say I was surprised at your request—so I talked it over with your mother. To determine what needed to be included." He looked off into the distance for a moment, his eye still. "Almost since the dawn of time, man has drawn maps, representing the way-finding urge. Those are lost, of course, hidden I suppose on the walls of caves or buried in mud or rock. In the civilized world . . ."

Roskins went on, not noting that the boy seemed momentarily lost in his own thoughts. ". . . Maps were an advance in human thinking—the ability to abstract, out of the current situation, the current view. Have you ever thought," Roskins said with sudden animation, "how a map allows you to know, to see, to locate, something invisible to you, something outside your range of vision?"

Now he had the boy's attention. "I never had."

"Like a kind of a glass to make an unseen object clear to the eye. A telescope. A microscope."

He opened the folder and brought out a sheet of paper. "This is only a reproduction—the original is in a museum somewhere."

"A reproduction."

"A copy. Now look at this." He slid the paper around so Richard could see what looked to be an awkwardly drawn sketch, with some areas colored in, and words written here and there. The sketch depicted various cities, with fields and trees and mountains around them; one of the cities was in the foreground, and the others were in the distance.

"This is an early attempt," said Roskins. "It's supposed to be a map of Tuscany, a part of Italy, but it's not really. Do you know why it's not really a very good, hardly a proper map at all?"

The boy shook his head.

"Because it's drawn—as a painting is—from the perspective of one viewer. Now, look at this."

Roskins drew out another sheet of paper from the folder and placed it between them. The paper shook; Roskins's hands were trembling—and the boy had never noticed that before, even though it may have always been so.

This paper depicted what looked like maps the boy had glimpsed—with little interest—in newspapers and textbooks. It showed an outline of Brittany, and there were roads and rivers crudely drawn on it.

"Here they've gotten it," said Roskins. "This is a real map—because it's not from one perspective. It's a map because a map is a view from nowhere."

"It's a view from nowhere?" said the boy.

As if Roskins unconsciously responded to some emotion he sensed in the boy, he spoke with sudden intensity. "Or from *everywhere*. A map is a view of an area from hundreds and hundreds of simultaneous perspectives—an infinite number, really—as if the uncountable eyes of God were looking down on the land, and laying out in a scheme exactly what was below them. Here now, look at this." He put another map between them, an early one, that had known areas detailed in, and unknown areas—lost continents and seas—marked with dragons and beasts.

They stared at it in silence as the boy ran his finger along a coastline and then out over the water.

"Now, if it's a proper map, it's quite easy to read," Roskins said. He lifted the sheet away and brought out two others. As the boy looked on with interest, the tutor went on to show how to relate a certain point on a map to another point, and how a grid was often laid on a map, with numbers and letters given for certain places that you could then line up and find. He briefly explained how keys worked, how distance was reduced in a ratio, how colors were used symbolically or pictorially.

"Now," said Roskins as he opened up the folder again and brought out another sheet. "Let's look at a detailed map of the city." The boy's heart quickened, as he took in the idea that a map could be a kind of spyglass or binoculars to make a part of the world unknown to him appear before his sight. He would know to look up the name in the index and line up its coordinates to find Hodge Lane and *battersea, battersea*. He would know the distance from the ratio, and the key would explain the obstacles, and then he would be able to do the way-finding that Roskins had said was part of that ancient urge that had led to such advances in thought . . .

Roskins swung the map around, and the boy in all his expectation—and with sweat in his palms, and his stomach uneasy—looked and didn't quite know what he was seeing.

"Here is the Coliseum," said Roskins, "and here is the Appian Way."

"This city—" blurted the boy. "I'm sorry, I don't—"

"The city of Ancient Rome," said Roskins. Then he put down the paper, and his hands fumbled together. "Your mother was most clear," he said, "that I have been charged only to teach you history."

~

All during luncheon with his mother—where she spoke of the proper ways to write letters of introduction or condolence—he felt restless, yet wary of appearing so. After they'd finished, and the dishes were cleared from the table, he returned to the room and strode about, in a large irregular circle, looking up at the farm and addressing the figures there.

I won't know where you've been if I can't get a map, he said. *You see, I'm not very good at these things. I know the greengrocer and the tailor shop, I know the few lanes to the stationery store—but beyond that . . .* He walked several paces away, then turned abruptly.

But do you think she's not talking to me the same as she used to? he asked. *Do you think it's different? You've been watching.* He suddenly felt a kind of panic, as if his world had been unaccountably shaken.

I'm not sure, said the woman in the window.

I think so, said Erin, in his taunting voice.

But different with her or you? asked Martin. *You're the one sneaking with the lamp, took that clipping, has a sickish feeling now you've eaten.*

Then maybe it's both of us, said the boy. *Maybe it's both of us who have changed. But what could have started it?*

A man at the door, a monkey in a gallery, said the woman in the window.

I'm the monkey in a gallery, said the boy angrily. *And hoboes have been here before.* As if to quell his remaining anxiety, he walked in another circle. He was speaking again: *I can't think about all that, it's a map I need, just a map of the city.* He paused a moment, thinking of maps. *Finding my way to the Coliseum won't help; I need a proper map. . . . But you can't give me one—there's nothing you can do, you only have one perspective on things. I need . . . I need other perspectives.*

He stopped at the end of the table and looked down at his

hands for a moment where they rested on its surface. He thought of how people said they knew things like the backs of their hands, but even his flesh there looked unfamiliar, pale, like something from the sea.

That's what I need, he said.

They didn't answer him. There seemed a change in them.

What is it? He whirled around and saw the cook, her cheeks red and her hair wet, and something—not a plate or utensil—in her hand. She jumped at his reaction, and cried out something in her language.

"What is it?" he said. "What do you want? How long have you been standing there?"

She smiled timidly and wiped her cheek with her hand. She was wearing the kind of dress that was called a jumper, over a white blouse buttoned to the neck. She looked younger, more like a schoolgirl being startled. She quickly lifted her arm, and held out what was in her hand.

"What is that?" he said, looking from the book she held to her eyes and back. Still she held it, and he hesitated. Then he walked forward and snatched it, and she flinched a little again. *"La Carte et le Guide,"* he read aloud. "It's in French. I don't understand it. I mean, it's most nice of you, but . . ."

He made to hand it back, and she lifted her head slightly, in a jerking motion, as if trying to show him what to do.

He jerked his head too, in an unconscious imitation of her, and she laughed. Red-faced, he looked down at the book. He opened it, began to flip through it. Pages and pages in a foreign tongue. Then his thumb caught on a thicker page, a flash of color. He opened it wide.

It was a map.

"Une carte," said the young woman. "A . . . map . . ."

"Of the city," said the boy. "Of this city where we are. Thank you. Very much. Most pleased. Sorry for—" He shook his head. Then, without thinking, he added, "I won't tell her." She continued with her slight smile, not understanding what he meant.

~

On a Wednesday his mother left the house. She would be meeting with some people from the newspaper where her column ran, and later in the day, supervising the week's shopping with the cook.

The boy watched from behind the glass of the doors, as she and Madeline walked down the gravel walk; Madeline gave him a shy smile before she turned and fell back into step. His mother opened the gate—and with a sinking feeling in his chest, he watched as they turned down the lane, and were gone.

He waited, counting to a hundred, and a hundred again. Then he too was crunching down the gravel walk, carrying the guidebook, and, as if he'd left a boy behind, imagining he was growing smaller from that boy's perspective.

He knew the first lane, and the second; he passed trees and fence posts that grew smaller or larger depending on how far he was from them, that were solid beneath his hand when he touched them. He passed other houses, like his own, set back from the cobblestone path, and now a few shops that he knew: greengrocer, tailor, stationer. These he looked toward, and was startled to see his own reflection striding past them in the glass.

This neighborhood where he lived, like a little village

unto itself, gave way to other streets and lanes; he stopped and looked this way and that, trying to match where he stood to the diagram in his hand.

The map was rather small, and tightly drawn, looking like a tangle of string. But he found himself; there he was, *there,* and it gave him comfort as he started down a lane he'd not yet been to, to think of himself as nothing but a little figure walking on a page.

He strode down an alley that widened until it became a street; houses on either side, bricks beneath his feet, shops with signs. He recognized an art store he'd passed in a carriage, with a small wooden mannequin seated in its window.

He turned onto another street, which corresponded to a thick bit of string, and he traced it with his finger. There were people about, moving every which way, coming from shop doors carrying packages, buttoning their coats or smoothing down their collars, speaking softly or loudly to one another; and horses, clopping along calmly. He caught himself staring at one with blinders.

The street widened again, and he kept along the right curb, along with the others who were going in his direction. The houses here were close against the street, and there were shops of various kinds, going up two and three stories, with lovely signs showing sheep and men smoking pipes and suits of clothes. When he looked again at the street, he felt he had grown smaller, as there were more people around him, and the buildings taller than he'd yet seen. There were unfamiliar smells of horses and smoke, and alien noises of horses' hooves and carriage wheels, of bells and the calls of vendors and snatches of music and shouts . . .

He quickly lowered his head and looked into the map, trying to see the way to Hodge Lane.

Someone pushed against him, and the book fell from his hand . . .

And as he knelt to pick it up, all that he had been trying not to see burst upon him. From his crouch—from the height of a much younger child—he saw the looming figures moving around him. He held the book, unable to stir; although there was a realistic fear that in his crouch he might be knocked over, it wasn't that which terrified him, which brought to mind the high-pitched crying of the horse. What frightened him, among the crowds of unfamiliar people, was somehow their coats and pants, their skirts and sleeves blowing in the breeze, seeming to flow together: The individual curls of cloaks and bonnets, shawls and scarves turned into wave upon wave as he watched, billows in a vast sea that threatened to cover him. He flailed with his arms, as if fighting to the surface, and a hand grabbed his shoulder, and he fought it off.

"Now, laddie," said a voice, and he pulled away, looking frantically around him, as if searching for help.

There was a girl in an advertisement on the side of a wagon. She was sitting so calmly at a table, beaming as she ate something from a bowl . . .

He clambered up onto the side of the wagon.

I beg your pardon, she said, *but you didn't knock.*

Don't you see? he cried. The steam from her bowl was painted in a gray wash, and he focused there, not on the street that the wagon was moving down. He only gestured there, without looking.

Nothing unusual now, she said, the spoon frozen halfway to her mouth, *except for your manners*.

He looked imploringly to her eyes: They were just painted blue dots, not even rendered that convincingly.

Just the regular street where we always go.

Just that?

Just that.

But I saw . . .

Yes?

He shook his head, and let himself look again. As they moved along the street, through the traffic, he was now able to pick out the distinct things that earlier had seemed to flow together so dangerously. Pedestrians were stopping to let the wagon through, while others were engaged in conversations as they walked. Coats and cloaks were only ruffling mildly in a breeze.

It's just the ordinary street, she said.

But I thought . . .

"Hey, you, boy," came a shout. "Get down from there." A red-faced man was yelling at him, and he dropped to the pavement. He stared up at the picture of the girl as the wagon rattled away.

You thought it was a shipwreck, she said.

Chapter 8

Hodge Lane was a narrow, quiet street of residences and shops, each attached to the next, with gas lamps along the walk. He traveled on the far side of the lane, on the odd-numbered side, not looking at anyone he passed, merely counting off one, three, five, seven, nine. At the final number, he turned and looked across the street; a horse and carriage was just passing in front of his view, and when it was gone, he saw Number 10.

It was indeed a gallery, where he could see the colors of propped-up canvases displayed in the broad window in front. As he stepped from the curb, he could spy in the room behind the window rows upon rows of paintings; as he walked toward them—not looking around, stepping ahead of another horse and trap—he felt he was flowing toward them on a sea of color.

It was perhaps this that allowed him to boldly walk in the front door of the shop, not thinking he was just a boy in some unknown area of town—his eyes were so filled with these portraits and landscapes.

A scene from the American West—a vast, empty plain, with diminutive horsemen and dots of buffalo crossing a river. A man in a dark jacket, with a red tie loosened at his neck; a woman with a coy half-smile, her face filling the frame; two girls with their arms on each other's shoulders, blonde-haired, in pink dresses. All with their dead eyes staring out. *Hello,* the boy wanted to say, but there were other people moving about the shop.

He walked along the wall of the room, looking up all the time. A valley in Germany; Portsmouth; a bearded man with a small gold crown on his head; a green bird with long legs on a white background. And now one that seemed blurred, yet at the same time had a familiarity about it: a portrait of a woman, young and lovely, dressed in blue, with a large hat, seated on a swing. He stopped before this one; he tilted his head . . .

"That's the monkey one," said a voice, and he turned. A young girl had her hand over her mouth, unsuccessfully muffling her laughter. She was in a blue jumper, had red hair in pigtails. "That's why everyone looks at it," she said.

"I'm sorry?"

"Because they saw it in the papers," she said, impatient now. "You were looking at it like—"

"Madeline!" called a voice from across the room.

"Your name is Madeline?" he said to the girl.

"Now, don't bother the customers," said the voice, which belonged to a red-haired adult woman sitting by a cluttered desk that had note cards strewn on top of it, as well as a large letter opener that was different from his mother's. She gave the boy a smile, and then stirred her tea and took a sip.

"Mum didn't want them to name our shop in the article, but I said it would be good for the business," said the girl.

The boy glanced again at the painting. It was the one he had read about in the clipping he'd found, and it was that which must have made it seem familiar.

There was a look of longing in the eyes of the woman, which he felt he could discern through the blurred paint.

The little tag beneath the painting said:

Blue Woman
F Jones

"It's always the title first," said the girl, noticing where he was looking. "I tell my mother that's the kind of thing you need to tell the customers, but she says, 'Well, they wouldn't think the painter was Blue Woman, now would they?' Mum doesn't know much about running the gallery. It's my uncle's, but he's off in Germany buying some dreadful pictures." She went into a whisper: "So it's really me that's minding the store."

"Madeline, leave that boy alone."

"Why do you blink like that?" she said.

"It's . . . your name. I know someone else."

"Who?"

"Someone I know. She's . . . French."

She smiled suddenly, and looked him up and down, stopping at the book in his hand. "Are you French?"

"Well." He hesitated, looking quickly around.

"Either you are or you aren't."

"Well, I am," he said.

"I hear that it's pretty there, and everyone drinks wine, and everyone is in fashion." She held the skirt of her jumper out and moved in a half circle.

"That's right," he said.

The ribbons of her hat were open at her neck. He could feel her longing, longing to speak to him.

"Did you want some help with something? Or whoever you're with?" It was the red-haired woman, Madeline's mother. She was standing there now; she draped her arm lightly on Madeline's shoulder, and the girl looked up eagerly at her.

"He lives in France, Mummy. And he did say that everyone drinks wine there."

"Well, that's nice. But I'm sure not everyone." Then she looked at the boy again. "And could I help you?"

"He's been looking at this one," said Madeline.

"I see. Well, it's a nice one, isn't it?"

The strength of his own voice surprised him. "If it wouldn't be too much trouble, you see I'm trying to trace a painting," he said. "To see where it was—before. My . . . my *aunt* must have bought it from here. But I need to find out where it was . . ." He trailed off, and then added softly, "In what place it was before. If it wouldn't be too much—"

"And your aunt is—"

"She's in France."

"I see. Well." She seemed slightly surprised, whether at his request or at the idea of him being a French boy, or perhaps at something else. Madeline just looked at him with her round eyes, her round brown eyes that darted over his face, seeing this and that about him, which made him shift as he stood. He glanced at the wall again: There was a half-smile on her face, and her eyes were so blue, blue like the sea, like her blue dress . . .

He followed the woman across the gallery floor; he noticed more about the room now: the paint peeling in places; the pictures stacked on the floor, leaning against the wall. And up above the paintings, high up on the wall, windows, some latched, some with their latches broken. Madeline was prattling on about what she called *Pressionism,* saying, "What they do in Pressionism is put in all sorts of dabs and bits of color," until they arrived at the desk.

"And why does your aunt wish to know?" the woman asked.

The boy shook his head; his earlier boldness was gone. He glanced down silently at the handwritten cards, at writing that was larger and more rounded than his mother's.

"I see. Well, then, what is the name of your painting?"

"*Farm Life.*"

"And the artist?"

"I'm sorry, I don't know."

"Well, let's check how he's listed these." The woman seemed not to know what to make of the boy, but she went ahead and drew together a handful of the notes, and squared them, like playing cards. He suddenly thought back to his mother flipping down the cards for War, showing him how to play Patience. Madeline was standing on one foot and then another. A little bell rang on the front door—it must have sounded when the boy entered, but he didn't hear it—and Madeline skipped toward the door and said, "Do you want to see the one the monkey looked at?"

"Madeline!"

Madeline's mother returned to looking through the note cards, and the boy watched the names of paintings flash by. Then he gazed around the gallery—more landscapes, two men on horses, some people on a picnic in a glade. He found himself back with the woman on the swing, staring at her indistinct image as if he were viewing it through raindrops.

Hello . . .

"Here we are," said the woman. She drew out a card and read it. "Why, you must have known," she said to the boy.

"I'm sorry, known?"

"That it was the same artist. As the one who did the painting you were just looking at." She glanced across the room, but the boy had already turned there again, to gaze at the blurry woman on the swing.

"See, it's on this card," she said, and it took a moment for him to bring his vision back. She had a little blue rectangle of paper laid on the desk that read:

B Woman
F Life
F Jones

"F Life," she said. "*Farm Life*. He has this unusual way of abbreviating, my brother does. And see, the first would be for Blue—*Blue Woman*. But where it was before . . ." She flipped the card over.

"Hello, here's some more. *Farm Life*; acquired, and two weeks later, sold again."

"When was that?" asked the boy, still looking across the room.

"Let's see. Nine years ago."

Nine years ago you moved here. You were such a little boy then.

"Who—who bought it?" he asked.

"Doesn't say," she said, then she glanced up at him. "Are you having me on? You just said your aunt has it—that's why you're trying to trace it."

"Sorry, I meant to say, who had it before?"

"I see. It doesn't say . . . Wait, here's another. Now, what's he done here?" She brought out another card from behind the first, that had only a few words written on it.

R Venus—S

"What's that?" asked the boy.

"I'm not sure. Another one, no doubt, but it doesn't even say who it's by. Perhaps the same artist, this F Jones person. And what the *S* means, I have no idea."

"R Venus," said the boy.

She squared the cards and sighed. "Still, I hope it was a help. Do tell your aunt to stop by—if she's . . . in this country again. We have other lovely things."

"I will," he said. "And thank you. Most kind. Ever so much."

He walked along the wall, passing a dog in point position, a series of horses and riders, some jumping, some standing as if for show.

Then he was by her again. He looked down at his brown shoes—they were shiny, for he hardly ever walked the streets. Now up at her.

She was so absolutely still on the swing, yet slightly indistinct, as if in motion.

"You keep looking at her," said Madeline, who had tired of greeting people at the door. "I wish you'd stop it. Here, look at this one."

She took a step, and stood before the picture of the long-legged green bird. "It's awfully nice," said the boy.

"Stop it," Madeline said again. She was right: His eyes had gone back to her.

"Excuse me, I had better go," he said, and started for the door, Madeline walking with him. This time, he heard the bell.

"Did my mother help you find what you wanted?" she asked. "She gets so confused when she has to take over here—you should just have asked me."

"She was most kind. She gave me some names," he said. They stood just in front of the shop. The light wasn't as bright as it had been; it may have been later than he'd thought.

"What names?"

"A painter, maybe two. F Jones. R Venus."

"Well, if it was me, and I wanted to find out about a painter, or a painting, about R Jones or F Venus, or John Q Public or what other paintings he's done besides that silly woman, do you know what I'd do?"

He was looking down at his shiny shoes.

"I'd go to the museum," she said. "That's what *I* would do, what anyone would do. My mother should have told you that, if you don't already know."

He could just see her face through the window—blurred in paint, wavy behind the glass, holding in her swing. Lost now, among the bird and the horses, the field and the gentleman and girls.

"I wish you'd stop looking," she said. Then, in a quieter voice, in a tone he hadn't heard from her before: "My mother thinks it's silly, but I do worry, since it happened once." She was looking where he was, through the window, at her indistinct face. "Sometimes I'm afraid that dreadful animal will come back."

Chapter 9

Using the map, he found his way back with only a few wrong turns, translating the *rues* to streets as he walked. He tried to tell himself that there was no need to worry, that his mother probably hadn't returned yet. But he knew if she was there, she would be concerned—disappearing like this had been grossly impolite. He attempted to concentrate on the story he would tell her, for he felt some indescribable need to cover what he'd done, and allow for other days he would want to be out in the afternoon.

He counted off a word for each step he took: *I shall want to be out days in the afternoon.*

He turned down the lane, and paused for a moment at the gate. He hardly ever saw their house in this way, from the outside, looking in.

He entered through the front door. Inside, it was quiet; he hadn't noticed before how everything in the foyer—and now as he walked, the hall and parlor, the side rooms—was in its set place, with no clutter or dust around. It had been different in the gallery: There was paint peeling on the walls, books stacked on the floor, note cards strewn this way and that. The bell on the door had tinkled, and the other Madeline had been dancing around. Here all was still, and everything seemed fixed in its place, limned and colored: the portrait that Roskins made at his lessons, his hands clasped together, his slight nod when he finished making a point; his mother outlined at her desk, and then sitting in the dining room, as if lifted from one place to the other like a cutout.

It was no wonder he could sometimes go into paintings. He lived in one.

There were smells of cooking now, and as he opened the door to the dining room, he expected to see Madeline there, setting out the four shiny plates, or brushing her hair back from her face. But the smells were from the kitchen beyond. His mother was sitting, quite still, with her eyes closed, at the head of the table.

He walked up and stood by her, waiting for her to look at him. The blow came so quickly, he almost didn't see it, almost didn't glimpse her hand flash out, palm open, to smack his face. It was only after he felt the smarting in his left cheek that he was able to register or remember the quick motion of her hand.

"I shouldn't have done that," she said quickly, getting up from her chair and coming to him. "Let me see."

He gingerly pulled his own hand away. She'd never hit him that he knew.

"It's just red. There now, please don't cry." She sat again.

"I won't," he said.

"I shouldn't have done it," she said. She rose from her chair and paced away, her hands working together, and then came back and was seated once more. "But who knew where you had got to?"

He was rubbing his hand over his cheek, looking up at the painting of the farm by F Jones, the way F Jones had made the fields rise and fall in the distance; and he was thinking, I know who painted you, and I know of your brothers or sisters, a whole family of paintings made by F Jones . . .

"Please look at me," she said. "Oh, lately you're looking away when I speak to you." She turned and stared at where he had been looking, and when she turned to him again, her face seemed ashen.

"Where were you?" she softly asked.

He remembered the story he had come up with, and he repeated it now, in a quiet, passionless voice. How the ball had bounced over the gate and into the yard, soon after she and Madeline had left, and how a young boy—just about Richard's age—had come to the gate and asked for it to be returned. And how since it was only polite, after Richard had returned it, the boy asked if Richard in turn would like to play with the ball with him. He lived not so very far away. And Richard had gone and they had had a nice time—the boy's mother had had playing cards, with interesting marks, interesting faces on the picture ones, and she had shown them to Richard. And then Richard had completely lost track of time.

"I see," said his mother when his long account was over. "I'm just so sorry." There were tears in her eyes, and the boy felt tears in his. "Now if we could please—please forget it. You mentioned cards," she said brightly. "Let's play cards." She got up abruptly and walked to the side table beneath the painting, opened a drawer, and brought out a deck. He wondered if she could sense how those in the painting were watching her; and being so close, if she would begin to hear the horse. She handed him the deck to shuffle.

It was a pack of transformation cards that a grateful reader had once sent her, so called because the suit signs formed parts of fanciful pictures.

"Remember these?" she said as he looked through them. On the six, the clubs made a pattern of six black horses, with thick necks and heads and tails. There were eight diamonds on hats in a crowd, a heart on a queen's chest.

He divided up the cards for Beggar Your Neighbor.

"Oh, fun," said his mother. "We used to spend hours."

"Yes," he said, turning them over—a four with spades for faces, a two of hearts that was a pair of red birds flying away.

But now the cards were turning into little blurry paintings.

"I shall want to be out days in the afternoon," he said. "To play—to play with the young man again."

She held a card in the air a moment before she dropped it. "Well, you'll simply tell me. Is he new here? One for the jack."

"Yes, he's a new boy. He's moved here."

"From?"

"From France," he said, without hesitating. "Two for my queen."

"My goodness," said his mother. "A regular stranger."

"Yes."

"Oh, look at this ace," she said. "One eye in the middle."

Like an infinite eye, he thought, a map-making eye; but he only said, "Yes."

"And his name?"

"Excuse me?"

"The boy's name, he must have a name."

He hadn't prepared for this. "F . . . Freddy."

Her right eye twitched.

"Freddy," he said. "Just Freddy."

"And no last name. He can't have been so impolite as to not tell you his last name."

"Freddy James."

There was just the slightest pause before she responded. "Well, as long as he's a nice young man, a polite young man." She smiled. "Three for the king. See how the club forms his helmet?"

"Oh, yes," he said. And they played through the deck.

When he got to his room, he sat on his bed for a moment, staring at the figures that watched mute from the windowsill. For a moment, he felt almost indistinguishable from them. Then he roused himself, and on the kind of small card on which he noted assignments, he wrote the following, adding answers or questions to each word he remembered:

F (Farm) Life
B (Blue) Woman
R (?) Venus—S (?)
F (?) Jones

He lay back on his bed, and his breathing calmed. F Freddy—that had been stupid. But what would it matter to her anyway, if he knew the name of the man who had painted the farm that was framed in their dining room? The same man who had painted . . . He saw her face again, for a moment, as if she were appearing on his wall, blurry still, framed by her filmy blue hat . . .

The vision disappeared, and there was just his white wall again, bare as a gallery that's been robbed.

He rubbed his eyes and rolled over onto his stomach, to look again at the guidebook. The streets were as confusing as a maze. *The museum,* she had said. That's where she would go. He needed to know the word in French, he would have to ask the French Madeline. And then he would find his way there, along this map made for strangers.

Chapter 10

The monkey was walking around, he was funny, he made him laugh. The monkey picked up the stick, licked its end, and the boy laughed and laughed. Now the boy and the monkey were standing in front of a woman. No, a picture of a woman. No, a woman, and the thing that made it confusing was the boy was painting her face, moving his arm, up and down, and up and down, and he was laughing, and the face of the woman was laughing, and the monkey was lifting and dropping the stick.

The boy woke with a start in his bed. He looked to the windowsill and saw the sailor figure. For some reason he didn't understand—for the imaginary scene in the dream upset him—he tried to recapture it by closing his eyes again. There was just darkness now, and the fading image of the wiry brown animal that must have been newly stimulated by his visit to the gallery.

He tensed where he lay, and stared up at the blank ceiling, as if waiting for another image to form itself there.

Before he left his room, he walked over and picked up the figure of the sailor. Weathered leather, stuffed with something. He put it to his nose and smelled it: a faint odor of salt, as befitting a gift from a sailor, from a father he couldn't remember.

He held the banister on the way downstairs, taking a few

steps and stopping, leaning against the X of his arms and looking down at the house he knew so well, the large white room, the square of the oriental carpet. He shuffled toward his place in the dining room. A fly was stationed on the roll that had been set out for him. When he came close, he could see that the insect's seeming stillness was in fact made up of hundreds of tiny jerky movements: little nervous steps this way and that, rubbing its front legs together, twitching its wings. He watched it for a moment, wondering if it felt safe or if its twitches were tics of fear.

He waved his hand and the fly buzzed away. He wasn't sure where his mother was: He hadn't heard her pen scratching, didn't hear the short snaps of her trimming in the garden. He reached for the pot of tea, and for the first time, looked up. He held the pot suspended in his hand, and his mouth formed into a half-smile. He held the pot there until it began to grow heavy, to burn his hand. It smacked a little when he set it on the table.

The painting of the farm seemed different.

Even from where he was sitting, he thought he could see small changes: The figures were larger, the horse less distinct, the river more in the distance.

He felt an emptiness inside, a clutch of fear, as he walked around the table and approached it.

Hello, he said, to Martin and the stable man. *Hello*. But he could see it was ruined—Martin was crouching, not kneeling, and the stable man was half turned away. There was a distinct, almost unpleasant look on the face of the woman in the window.

Hello, hello, he said again.

There was no response.

He thought how if you didn't look that closely at it—if you hadn't studied it, if you hadn't *visited* it—you might not immediately register the difference.

After looking this way and that, he lifted it from the wall, and brought his head around.

FARM LIFE
BATTERSEA GALLERY
10 HODGE LANE

It was the same label, the identical ticket—ticket that was the origin of etiquette—only perhaps slightly curled away from the wood . . .

He stared at the painting again.

Hello, hello, hello, he tried.

He walked back to his chair. The fly had once again landed on his roll, and he didn't chase it away. For every little movement of its legs, he felt a hair rising on the back of his neck. If he was really right, and it somehow was a different one, then something must have happened to the first. And that could mean . . . It could mean that it hadn't just been something in the past that had frightened the horse.

It was something in the present as well.

He didn't speak to his mother about what he thought was the change in the painting, and neither did she make mention of it. He would walk in the room and study it. The shade of the grass seemed different. No, it was the same. No, it was different. It was slightly smaller in its frame. No, he was just farther back. He was the same distance away.

And how could there be two paintings of this same farm, this ordinary subject? And where was the first one?

He tried to understand it. He had hidden things from her—his looking at the clipping, the gallery visit, the note card in his room—and perhaps this was how she had paid him back. Then that wasn't so odd, he thought, it was just her way of teaching him to be polite. Or maybe something had happened to the first one, and she hadn't wanted him to be upset. And so she'd found this other. Or maybe the painting itself had somehow changed. But beyond all these shifting thoughts there remained the fact that it was she who must have changed it, and it made him understand that his strange behavior in not telling her things was based on some instinct or wisdom that he didn't have full access to, that in sneaking around like a thief he was in some way protecting himself, while at the same time opening up a world that seemed fraught with danger.

The next afternoon he was again sitting in the dining room, but this time his back was to the painting. He didn't want to look at it, and blink, and look at it again. Instead, he was facing the blank wall opposite, munching on some bread that had been put out for him, for early tea. His mother was in the little sunroom with guests, and once again he heard their voices, their laughter rise and fall. If his mother's laughter was part of it, he could not pick it out.

As he stared at the wall, he thought again about Martin and the horse, and tears sprang to his eyes. And then, before him on the white expanse of plaster, as if it were a cryptic solution to this puzzle, another scene formed itself before his eyes. He was glimpsing the ocean—white with froth—in the throes of a mythological storm. He saw pale waves rippling, and in the sky above them, the most wonderful objects were tumbling down to disappear forever—women and beasts, angels and ships, and a farm, yes, a farm—as if torn from the sky by some god, and hurled to the trembling sea below.

After a moment, his vision cleared. The wall was just the wall again.

He turned around in his chair. The painting was different. He laid his head in his hands, and closed his eyes, refusing any more to see.

~

After the guests left, he went and sat in the sunroom, among the plates and cups still on the table, the earthenware pot as familiar to him as an old friend. He picked up the guidebook in his hand, and then gently put it down on the table before him. They'd had little cakes; they'd had those lovely sandwiches without crusts. Sometimes after he had played cards with her, they would have tea, and sometimes tea before and cards after. He remembered the cupid on the back of a little spoon. She'd danced it around for him while he drank his milk and hot water. He remembered what she'd said sometime long ago: *Now we'll take our tea. We'll pour the milk in. We'll butter the bread. See, you're taking tea like a big boy. Look, you can eat all that bread . . .*

Through the back window, he looked out on the lawn. There was another house behind it, through some trees, that he'd never paid much mind to. Now he wondered who lived there.

He heard a footfall and turned. Madeline came into the

room, walking purposefully, carrying a tray, dressed in an apron that was over her jumper. She smiled when she saw him, and standing by the table where he was sitting, she started to put the tea things on the tray.

His heart sped up. He watched her thin hands shifting the cups and saucers, and as she turned to go, he opened the guidebook to the map in the back. From his pocket, he brought out a note card and laid it down on the map. He had written the word *museum* on it, and pointed now to the word. "Oh, *musée,*" she said with a laugh, and took his finger and traced it along the page to a large square and building, where that word was printed. She laughed again, and turned away with the tray. He took a bit of cake she'd left and put it into his mouth, letting its sweetness linger as he stared at the map.

It wasn't too long after she'd gone that the fly buzzed in the room. It made several circles, and then it landed near his arm, and skittered around the table, making its tiny jerky movements. Just as it took off, he struck out his hand and stunned it in the beginning arc of its flight. He was amazed at the quickness of his movement, the way he could cause it to lie there absolute and still.

The next was a clear, chill day; clouds skimmed across the sky, and Richard, watching them through the glass in the door, thought how they really were flying away from his squared area of viewing and appearing over other parts of the city: over the streets and the omnibuses, and over 10 Hodge Lane, where the woman and Madeline might be seeing them.

And the clouds were going over other places as well.

He told his mother he wanted to spend the afternoon with the French boy Freddy James. He could see her from the doorway as he asked, sitting at her table, tapping her pen, a stack of sealed letters before her. She nodded, and when he turned to go, she called him back.

"'Please.'" She spoke to him where he stood at the doorway.

"Please," he said into the room. "Of course."

"It's a convention we take for granted," she said. Then she shook her head, and he thought a faint smile came to her face. "You've given me the lead I've needed," she said. "All these letters, all these squabbles. I've been thirsting for something different. For my column this week. And I have it now, I have it. How the word *please* became such a part of common, polite speech. How often it saves the day, don't you think? And of course there's the other sense: to please someone. 'I won't do it if it won't please you.'"

It struck the boy as odd the way she was speaking to him through the room. And then, as if it were a wave, a frightening awareness burst over him: It *was* odd the way she was speaking, her discourses *had* grown increasingly strange. It wasn't only that *he* had wandered away. He reached out and held the door frame to steady himself.

"Of course, since you've asked so nicely, you can go. Go and play with the French boy."

He managed to respond with, "Thank you. Most kind."

If she registered the shift in him, he couldn't tell, for she had turned back to her desk.

He left with *La Carte et le Guide de la Cité* in his hand and money in his pocket that Madeline had lent him. He had promised he would pay her back someday, and she had shrugged. He walked again down his lane and noticed the differences here as well: A few leaves were now skipping in front of him that hadn't been there before; something had happened to one of the fence posts—it was tilted at a slight angle, and had a gash in its weathered wood.

He waited with a small group of people for an omnibus. Their seeming boredom at this routine contrasted with his fear and excitement—he had never ridden one alone. His heart again raced as the large conveyance approached, pulled by horses, with the driver on top in his hat and cape and gloves. He watched carefully as they handed the conductor their fares, and as closely as possible he tried to mimic their movements and nonchalant attitudes. He found a worn leather seat as the vehicle took off with a jerk. He avoided looking at the others: those who sat across from him in their hats and bonnets, those who staggered down the aisle like sailors when the vehicle slowed or accelerated. Sometimes they would pass an intersection and he would see in the distance other intersections, and others beyond, seemingly going on forever, with so many movements of horses and carriages, hackneys and pedestrians near and far that his eyes couldn't twitch fast enough to take them all in.

"Museum," Roskins had told him, "means 'home of the Muses.'" He had listed them for the boy: Erato, Muse of love poetry; Melpomene, of tragedy . . . the boy couldn't remember the others. They had lived, according to Roskins, on the mountains of Helicon, Pierus, and Olympus, among clear waters, grottos, and grasses dappled with

flowers, where sickness and death and terror had no place.

Although he could not remember if Roskins had used the word *terror*.

When the bus stopped at a place whose streets matched those in French in his little book, he quickly got up and walked toward the front, and down the steps to the avenue. He saw it before him, and he tried to fix his eyes on it as he walked toward it, through the bustling crowds. A flock of doves took off from the square opposite, circling around statues of lions, rising past a man on a pedestal. As he walked toward its pillared Greek facade, he did feel he was approaching another world, where Muses or those inspired by them might rest and pursue their gentle arts.

The museum was larger than he'd expected, and a mathematical equation came to mind—that the museum was to the gallery as the gallery was to the farm painting that had been in the dining room. For as he entered its first room, as he glimpsed room beyond room beyond room of paintings, he was struck with the amazing possibilities that lay around him. He had come to look for names of a painter, or painting: *F Jones, R Venus*. And he would. But all around him there was so much else to see: multitudes of frames that were windows into other worlds and times; so many paintings, they functioned like a map of multiple perspectives on the world. He walked down a corridor that offered a giddy selection of figures and scenes, of landscapes and periods of history.

Beyond the quiet viewers who in ones and twos were making their way slowly through the galleries, he glimpsed angels in clouds, armies that were battle-ready, ships floating serenely in harbors. Men and women were drinking, gambling, bowling; there were Arabs on horses, queens on thrones, women with halos, children playing in gardens, couples kissing and dancing while nymphs and fairies joined hands around them. And the faces: old, young, sad, smiling, pinched, and smooth. He saw armies clashing, knights spouting blood, saints losing their heads, deer scampering, boars raging, serpents writhing. As he walked from room to room, past the golden frames, he could almost begin to hear the cries and battle trumpets, the polite conversations, the sounds of lutes and pianofortes, thunder and heavenly choirs, sighs and moans and laughter. Music and laughter!

He felt at home here, at peace; it was so unlike the street visible through the glass, from which he had just come, and from which he now averted his eyes.

His thoughts were interrupted by a voice that echoed around him. *Hello*.

It took a moment to see where he was, and who was speaking. He remembered vaguely having caught in the corner of his eye a certain painting—and yes, that was where he was now. In front of him, a knight on a white charger was lancing in dreadful fashion the eye of a dragon, and blood was pouring from the dragon's head. Just to the beast's right, a young woman in a red dress was standing, holding a cord wrapped around the dragon's neck.

The boy walked toward the tableau of the three figures. He was in a strange, symbolic landscape, with twisted clouds above him, and blasted earth and unreal mountains in the distance.

It's quite wonderful that you should visit us, said the voice, which belonged to the woman.

Oh, yes, said the armored young man on horseback.

You see, said the woman, *they've all been outside, looking in. But you're on the inside, looking out.*

Yes, said the boy, *I can do that. But I wonder why I've started with you?*

You're such a boy, said the woman. She gestured toward the man in armor. *Don't you know who he is?*

I'm sorry, I have no idea, said Richard, studying the knight. Then, after a moment, he said, *I've got it! St. George.* St. George and the Dragon! *Roskins taught me about you!*

Very good, said the young man, and there was even a disgruntled snort from the dragon.

So of course you'd want to visit, said the woman.

Oh, yes. I mean . . . because . . . he faltered.

Because every boy who comes here, who's taken here by his nanny or his parents, imagines being like me, said St. George. *Being a knight in armor! Slaying his enemy! While the beautiful maiden looks on!*

Why, thank you, said the young woman.

So of course you're here, St. George continued.

Yes, said Richard, but with little enthusiasm. *Slaying his enemy . . .*

You know, I'm not sure, said the young woman after a moment. There was a trace of disappointment in her voice.

I'm sorry. Not sure? asked Richard.

If you are like other boys, said the maiden.

Oh, I am, said Richard. *I most truly am. I've been in school with other boys. And it is wonderful to be here. To imagine myself . . . To see myself in . . .*

No, said the young woman. *I think not.*

As if to further his argument—and to get away from these tiresome figures—he spied in an adjoining room another adventurous painting and headed there. Almost immediately, he found himself in a raucous scene of people outside a tavern, young men playing a kind of bowling game on the lawn, other men looking on, and a man and a woman—who was drinking beer from a glass—sitting on the grass.

But of course the young men weren't really playing the bowling game. The young man in the posture of releasing the ball was, expectedly, frozen. The game would never commence, and the two older gentlemen in unusual wide hats and dark cloaks would never step up and take a turn.

The boy glanced back at the dragon painting. See, I've come adventuring here, he wanted to say.

He turned to the figures near him. *What is this game you're playing?* he boldly asked one of the gentlemen in hats.

Ah, and who might you be?

A visitor, said Richard. *And the name of the game?* he demanded.

Skittles, said the young man, whose arm was slanted forward to release the ball. *Very popular here in the Netherlands.*

The Netherlands?

Yes.

But you speak English.

Of course—we've had lots of practice.

Practice?

From all the visitors.

I see, said Richard.

Some of them say the rudest things.

Well, I won't. Even though I'm a kind of visitor too.

Are you a traveler? asked the woman on the lawn. Her voice came out muffled, being spoken as it was into the glass she was holding to her face.

Some call me a mover, said Richard.

Ah, to move, said the boy holding the ball. *'Course, even if I could move, there's nothing to shoot at.*

Richard looked down the lane where the skittles player was aiming, and much to his surprise, he could see that he was looking at—well—nothing. The rest of the skittles court was not pictured; the painting was designed to be interrupted by its frame. So there was the unusual perception of a large piece of wood sticking out of the bowling court, with nothing visible beyond.

Out there, said the woman who could never drink the beer. *Out there's other worlds. I guess you've seen them.*

Yes, I have, said Richard. *I've seen . . .* He paused a moment. *So many places.*

And you just a young man, said the woman.

I'm actually only a boy. Just like any other boy . . .

Now, these other worlds, said one of the men in hats. *Where would you go to see them?*

Why, they're all around you. I'm visiting one and the other, you see, because I'm trying to find . . . well, I'm just visiting, that's all.

But they seemed less interested in his particular journey than in the information he had imparted. They began talking all at once, and he finally interrupted.

Can't you see, across the room, through that doorway? That dragon, that man on the horse? He peevishly left out mentioning the maiden. *And right next to you, there's a rather desolate field—I shouldn't go there—and down the corridor there's the interior of a tavern, and some finely dressed people walking through a park, and, oh so much!*

Really?

It's quite wonderful.

We have heard rumors, said the woman, whose voice was echoing around her beer glass. *The visitors, looking us over, talking about our color, our time. Then mentioning others, compared to us—*

Mentioning us as I said in quite a rude way, interjected the skittles player.

But we can never see the others, continued the woman.

Richard was slowly understanding: Their view of things was terribly broken up, tragically limited.

He suddenly had a mad urge to introduce them to one another. If they couldn't see, at least they could speak across these spaces. He prompted the skittles players to call out, until they were answered by voices from across the gallery. He felt quite happy for a moment as the figures made contact with one another, like explorers, sailing off the map into a new world, but finding something like home. However, as if they were people from different cultures, they introduced themselves in a funny way.

Uccello, said St. George. *Italian school. Fifteenth century.*

Jan Steen, said a chorus of voices from the skittles painting. *Dutch school. Seventeenth century. Oil on canvas.*

Us, too.

But you're quite early.

Yes, but he was a master, said the Uccello canvas. *So we look much later.*

Well, Steen was a master as well. I must say, I'm not sure about his use of perspective in you, at such an early stage.

Actually, said the Uccello, *we're quite ahead of our time.*

The boy left them in the midst of this conversation that was turning heated, as they continued to recite facts from the little tags affixed on the walls next to their frames. He left just as the boy playing skittles was saying that although the Italian school may have understood perspective, they little understood the unifying uses of light; and the dragon, speaking for the first time, begged to differ. Richard told himself he was moving on not because of this growing clash but because he did, after all, have something to find out.

But rather than look at tags for the names he was seeking, he stopped next in the interior of a tavern, where it appeared a wedding was under way.

The room was filled to overflowing, crowded with musicians and drinkers and people eating pies from a tray. It seemed made up of peasants from some earlier time—perhaps they were also Dutch—but what was most important to the boy was that he had never been in a tavern, never seen a wedding, and now here he was! He moved among the figures, who were saying things like *Hoooo hoooo!* as they held their jugs of beer aloft.

The bride, however, seemed out of sorts.

I don't like this setup at all, she whispered as he approached. *I'm here, but the man I've married is down there.* The boy saw the dilemma at once: As the groom had been painted at the other end of the table from her, there he would stay. They would never touch.

It ain't a right thing, for a woman such as me to be left alone, she continued.

I should say not, said Richard.

They say you're a mover, she said.

Oh, yes, he said, *that I am.*

Maybe you could come sit here by me? she asked.

I think I could, he answered after a moment, laughing. *I could because I'm a mover.* He felt like taking a tankard of ale. He picked his way over the table, and sidled up next to her and laughed again. But for some reason his arms were shaking. He looked to her: She had the same dough-faced expression. And now around him: It was the same simple scene, the peasants drinking, eating the pies; the groom almost out of the picture. But now it somehow made him uneasy.

He moved away.

He went into the scene of an extraordinary battle that was strange and familiar at the same time. Armies of knights were clashing—that is, were about to clash: swords raised, trumpets at puckered lips, horses rearing and ready to charge. In the foreground a man with a pike was about to bring it down on the arm of his enemy. And the boy could walk among this frozen moment of battle—as he had done at the boisterous, unhappy wedding—at his leisure. He could inspect the twisted faces of the soldiers, the flaring nostrils of the horses, as if walking among a field of the dead. He saw that some of these figures looked similar to the man on horseback with the dragon.

Uccello? he queried, and everyone in the battle, knight and horse, trumpet and flag, responded with a resounding *Yes!*

You're all Uccello?

Yes! Uccello!

And where am I?

You're in a masterpiece! they cried.

Oh, yes, said the boy. He walked among them awhile longer, as if he too were waving a magnificent sword in his hand—waving it boldly, this way and that, and dreaming of slaying his enemy—as any boy might.

Chapter 11

He kept circling around her, visiting other paintings but often looking over at her as he did, even through doorways. He was exploring strange and wondrous places, so why should he trouble himself with her? He'd hardly been on the shore, and now he could walk far out along a strand, somewhere near Calais. He'd hardly call himself a lad who was comfortable in society, but now he walked amidst the decorous couples of someone named Watteau, men and ladies lounging in a softly lit park, who exclaimed when they saw him and asked if he too found the afternoon as enchanting as they. He'd hardly gone to church, yet now he was visiting a saint who was witnessing a miracle: a crucifix appearing between the horns of a deer. This rather haggard individual blessed him as he appeared, and asked him if his miraculous arrival was part of His Divine Plan.

The boy realized that paintings were from one perspective in another way as well: Everyone in them assumed that he fit into their particular scene, and gave little thought to what other purpose he might have.

He didn't *feel* like visiting the painting of the woman—this woman who was sitting by the side of a dark pool, with her head in her hands in a posture of eternal weeping, this woman who had obviously just read the letter that lay in the grass at her side, this woman in the white dress with the fallen lilies drifting from her, seated as she was among the drooping branches that were so obviously reflective of her mood.

Yet he found himself by her side, looking past her into the pool that didn't glisten, but was rendered in some flat brown oils, listening to her quiet crying.

Disappointed Love, he said, reading the name tag. *Francis Danby. British school.*

He faltered suddenly. *I'm sorry—you see, I don't know why I've come.*

My heart is broken, said the young woman, with her head in her hands.

He stood a moment by her side, waiting for her to go on. As he understood she must.

I didn't want to know, she said. *I didn't want to read the letter. I knew it would trouble me too much. Cause too many feelings within me.*

You wanted to leave things as they were, said the boy.

Yes.

You didn't want to open up unforeseen consequences.

That's correct. And yet I felt compelled to.

Compelled to . . .

To see, she said through her hands, into her tear-soaked white dress, by the lilies that were forever just out of reach and drifting away on the water.

I've been visiting places, he said. *Wonderful places. Battles, weddings.*

Battles and weddings, she said, and seemed to cry even harder.

I don't really know about them, he said softly. *You see, even though I am a mover—I'm just a boy.*

You do know about them, she said.

I don't think—

It's like the letter, she said, *that's lying behind me on the bank. I didn't want to open it. And you—it's as if you've forgotten why you're here, that you don't want to open—*

I'm here as any other boy might be, he interrupted.

She didn't respond; she let his own voice echo over the brown pool, to ring falsely back at him. Finally, she did speak: *In the gallery next to me. You glanced in—and then you quickly left. Do you remember why?*

It's funny, I almost didn't remember doing that. He paused. *It's because of what I saw,* he said.

What did you see?

I saw—I saw a woman, looking at her reflection.

Was that all?

He paused a moment, as still as she. And in that stillness, he understood that he needed to go into that room.

All right then, I will, he said.

Before he turned to go, he added, *I'm sorry your heart was broken.*

She spoke again. *I am sorry too. About yours.*

He would go into the room, but not into the painting; he would just stand before it. He walked past a Madonna and child, past a crucifixion. There were a few other people in the gallery: a young man, sketching, and a man with gray hair in a dark brown suit and a woman with a cane and shawl walking slowly from frame to frame. Their murmuring voices drifted over him, pleasing him; he thought people who visited museums were as decorous as the stilled images on the wall.

The painting was of a woman, lying across a couch after her bath, her back toward the viewer. A figure was bracing a glass, in which she could see her lovely face . . .

It was an angel holding a mirror.

He wouldn't go into it, he would only look up at it. As he once had. Once.

The murmuring figures passed behind him, the woman using her cane, the man quietly shuffling. The young man left the gallery carrying his pad.

Don't you remember, said the angel, *how you used to look up at me, and talk to me?*

Yes.

You pretended you were sitting on the couch with me.

I felt I was sitting on your couch.

You were so little then.

Oh, yes, when I was so little. Did I somehow come here?

You talked to me. You went la la la, you went ba ba ba. And then you said things. And you talked to the others too.

The others?

Oh, yes. The others that were with us.

He looked around at the paintings on the walls.

These?

Don't you remember?

No.

You can.

I don't remember.

You can be with them again if you wish.

And when I do—will I know what's troubled you all?

You were such a little boy then, the angel said.

Nine years ago, said the boy. *Was that when I was a little boy like any other?*

Oh, yes, then you were a little boy like others.

He looked from the angel to the woman's face. *I used to talk to you too,* he said. *Was it you? I think it was you. I used to want to be with you.*

Yes, you did, she said. *But there were unforeseen consequences.*

The painting being changed—that was one?

Oh, we were all changed, said the woman. *Just a little, not too much. People thought it a nice touch.*

It wasn't scary? said the boy.

Not those changes, said the angel, *those were fun. The scary ones came later.*

The boy looked down, then up at the woman. *Are those ones coming again?*

Yes, she said. *If you want.*

And although nothing had shifted in her expression, he understood that she had grown terribly sad.

He took a step back from the painting and looked at its ticket: *Diego Velázquez, Spanish school, oil on canvas.* And then its title: *The Rokeby Venus.*

R Venus.

He shot a look back up at them—but now they were still, quiet, just figures in paint. They wouldn't be able to help him now, to tell him how he could have come here to this museum room those years ago. Or why their name was on a card in a gallery where a beast had been found, or why his mother had cut out a clipping about it to read and read again. They could only look out at him with their sad and compassionate eyes. The same as the blurry woman in the swing.

Chapter 12

He found himself walking aimlessly from the museum, choosing one street and then another, until the crowds of people and the teams of clattering horses diminished. He had been walking a good hour when he turned onto a slightly graded stone street, heading downward. It was easy to walk here, and he let his footsteps take him, one before the other, seemingly of their own accord. He passed a cluster of brick houses with small courtyards, one where a child with a dirty face stared at him as he walked past.

When he emerged from the houses, a breeze caught him. He heard the piercing cry of a gull, and saw a wide ribbon of slate blue: He'd walked to the river.

Beyond a stone road and a grassy strand, there were ships passing, some billowing smoke, some with sails taut in the wind, and men walking about the decks. Just before him, a narrow dock extended where more small boats were tethered. These had bells on their masts and spars that rang each time the crafts shifted in the current.

He hadn't been this close to the water as long as he could remember, and yet, for some reason, he felt little fear. He paused as he looked down at the scene—and then he let himself walk closer.

The ships sailing by on the river, one with smokestacks

pulling a barge, made curls of waves where they moved through the water.

And the ships with their bells ringing . . .

Looking at the river now, he remembered another water scene, different from that staged at the theatrical. This one was a harbor: Little men were rowing out in boats to a ship that was anchored just off shore, its sails being hoisted. There were other men on the bank; there were strange buildings on the far shore.

He couldn't remember.

You can if you wish, the angel had said.

He opened his eyes, watched the boats skimming by. Closed them, saw the harbor in his mind's eye, and how everything there was still—the little boat, and the boat with sails, the sails themselves, even the water . . .

He opened his eyes. It was moving. He closed his eyes. It was still.

"It's another painting," he said aloud.

He closed his eyes again, and he could see it more clearly. The little men in the boats had funny hats. Like the hats in the skittles painting.

Netherlands hats.

Now the boy was standing in front of a woman. No, a picture of a woman. No, a woman, and the thing that made it confusing was the boy was brushing her face, moving his arm, up and down, and up and down, and he was laughing, and the face of the woman was laughing, and the walrus was moving its head. No, it was a tall man, with a mustache like a walrus's, and sticking-out teeth, and the tall man was standing in front of a painting and laughing. And the little monkey was scampering around on his thick bowed legs and the boy walked from the woman over to the painting where the man was and saw the face of a woman who was laughing. She was sitting on a boat. Under a Netherlands hat.

He woke up then, his heart pounding, alone in his room, the figures looking at him from the windowsill just figures—and he was alone. He closed his eyes. He wanted to see her face again, and then he did, and it made him sit up suddenly, and gasp for breath.

He *had* seen that face before.

He went down to breakfast in the same white shirt he had worn the day before, sat before the teapot and his roll, glancing up at the painting of the farm. When Madeline came in to see if she could clear away the breakfast things, he took out *La Carte et le Guide de la Cité,* and held it out, not offering it to her, but holding it between them as an object of mutual observation. He hesitated a moment as he recalled the phrases he had studied in the little glossary in the back, the few simple words he had gone over and over.

She brushed her bangs from her forehead and looked at him.

"Merci," he said, *"pour le livre. Il est un très bon livre. S'il est possible, j'ai besoin de ça. S'il vous plaît."*

She flashed him a smile at the unexpected words, and in some kind of seeming excitement said back something rapidly that he didn't understand. Then she blushed, and repeated her words slowly, first in French, and then in halting English. "Yes . . . it is all right."

She waited a while longer, as if to hear him once more

speak in these words of her homeland, that the boy suddenly understood must have such power for her, the phrases that had been said back and forth by her *mère* and *père* when she was a little girl, when she was just a little girl like any other and lay in her bed and looked up at the blank ceiling above her and heard words like these.

"Merci," he said again as the whole room blurred. *"Merci pour le livre."*

He stood for a moment outside the doorway of the drawing room. He looked at his mother, sitting there among the stacks of envelopes that seemed more numerous today, that were clustering around her like the leaves that were falling outside the window, as she sat with her letter opener on the desk before her. He called to her and she seemed not to hear him, and he called again, speaking to a statue and telling it he was going out to play again with the French boy Freddy James, after he had his lesson with Roskins. As he started away, what came to mind was the painting of the woman he had visited, who was sitting before the pool with the letter opened at her side and her head in her hands silently weeping.

He went upstairs and hesitated here as well. There was a rushing sound in his ears, that slowly became more distinct—syllables, words, now phrases. Rules and rules of propriety ran through his head; how crossing one foot over the knee was not acceptable in society; how boys should treat their mother as politely as if she were a stranger who did not spend her life in their service . . . He knocked three soft times on the door, and when there was of course no response, he pushed against it and felt it give, as the voices rose into shouts and then, when he shut the door behind him, grew suddenly silent.

He stood there, in this room of white and silence: his mother's room. He saw the freshly made bed and the vanity in white wicker. In his white shirt he told himself he was just an added stroke of white, a layering of pigment, barely able to be seen. But he was a jagged streak, a rude mark flashing in the mirror, and one that moved in the most unexpected ways, as he dropped to the floor and looked beneath the bed, felt behind the wicker vanity, and raised his hand with a sudden urge that scared him, to send spilling the delicate bottles there and make stains all around.

It wasn't hard to find. He supposed he should have been listening for her footsteps on the stairs, or preparing to beg her forgiveness, but he began to feel as he had in the paintings, reckless and beyond caring, beyond stopping. He brushed aside a handful of dresses and pulled out a small box that was set against the back of her closet. It was there, behind it. He could see the edge of the green field, the tiny head of the horse. Even though he'd felt certain she'd changed it for the other, his actually finding it here felt like a blow inside him, equivalent in force to the smack she'd given him on his face.

And why, he wondered, why, if she wanted to fool him, would she do it in such an obvious way, and hide the original in such an easily discovered place? Was it just a funny game, like the tricks she'd once done with cards, the queen vanishing, only to reappear? It didn't seem that; it seemed more the way you would deal with someone you expected would never trust what he'd seen, and certainly not think to look in obvious places. Someone who was just so frightened, so uncomprehending, as restricted as a figure in a frame . . .

He opened the box first. It was an ornate jewelry case, with green scallops and red flowers, and had his mother's name, Abigail Foster, engraved on its cover. Inside, there were folded pieces of paper. He pulled out the first.

> *There was a humorous incident in one of the shops in the gallery district. Upon opening, a monkey was found within, staring dumbly at one of the paintings. The clerk who failed to lock the door was summarily sacked and . . .*

He refolded it, and picked up the next, which was partially ripped

> *. . . not much of worth has been taken: frames, paints, brushes, of value estimated at not over 15 pounds.*

And the next:

> *Prints and framing supplies have been reported missing from several galleries in the Battersea section, on Hodge Lane and bordering. Asked if any of the prints reported missing were of much value, Mr. Ferguson, a shop owner, said, in a word, no; they were slightly altered reproductions, meant to have an amusing or disorienting effect. Once in fashion, they were now no longer in demand and had in fact been pinched from the back storage room where they'd been relegated. Someone could have bought the lot for less than 20 pounds, he estimated.*

He returned the clippings to the box. As he was closing it, he noticed something else, sticking out just a little from an embroidered pocket on the inside of the cover. It took sharp eyes to see it at all. He reached for it and plucked it out: It was a 50-pound note, folded in three. With unaccustomed motion, his thoughts scrambled ahead: Twenty and fifteen were only thirty-five . . . So if she had fifty pounds at her disposal, it wouldn't be she who had stolen a lot that totaled thirty-five.

He took a breath and replaced the bill, closed the box.

He walked over to the closet, reached back inside it, and carefully lifted out the painting, bringing it through the clothes that trapped it for a moment. During her theft—or maybe in his recovery—paint had been chipped away, leaving a white spot in the field behind the barn. He was relieved that the horse wasn't looking in that direction; but he felt that the others knew, and that he would have to calm them—even Martin—and try to repaint it with the watercolors when he had a chance. But in the light of that white room, with the painting propped on his knee, the figures didn't seem at all lifelike to him; he could see the minute jagged way their painted faces met the pigmented background of the field and road and fence.

As he turned the painting over, something brushed his legs and he jerked the frame away. Then he calmed, and studied the back. The label was gone, as he knew it would be, for it had been imperfectly attached to the new painting that was hanging. No, it was the cord that had surprised him: The cord that had held the frame to the hook in the wall was broken, and its two tattered ends dropping from their little posts were what had touched his legs.

He understood better why the figures had seemed flatter and more . . . withdrawn. They must have been frightened once again. For it appeared that the painting had been pulled from the wall with sudden and unexpected force.

~

It all made sense to him now. He understood how the catastrophe, the terrible crime against civilization, had occurred. It was, he supposed, what he needed to know for his final examination—parallel to the examinations that boys and girls were given at school or university, these students he glimpsed on the street with their book bags and jackets and caps that they tore from each other's heads. He explained it all very clearly to Roskins: how the seeds of civil unrest, and the poorly administered government, and the various emperors and caesars who had gained notoriety for their cruelties and betrayals, and the difficulties of course in keeping such an overextended empire functioning—not to mention the various hostile tribes that were able to wage wars—all contributed to a massive upheaval, chaos, Rome overrun, burning and looting in the streets.

"Well, yes," said Roskins. "Exactly."

Richard had done so well in his reading, in fact, that there was time before they started on their next area of learning, when the boy could study something else of his choosing. This was something that Roskins liked to do for all his students. "As long as," Roskins added, "it has a historical bent. Like when we looked at the maps. Boys often choose knights, or ancient battles, or . . ."

"Painting," said the boy.

"Painting?" The man appeared baffled.

"Historical paintings, of course. Masterworks. There couldn't be any objection from my mother. There are some I had in mind that I wish to learn more about. One in particular I was thinking of. Dutch, maybe seventeenth or eighteenth century. Ships in a harbor, just as the sun is rising. And . . . little men in boats."

"Dutch paintings. Of boats." Roskins's eye was fully twitching now. "I've never heard—"

"You said something of my choosing," said the boy.

"Well," said Roskins, thinking, "I suppose I can't see the harm in it. I'll have to find . . . Dutch, you say?"

"Yes. Of a harbor," said the boy. "And some of the men—have these Netherlands hats."

Chapter 13

She was waiting for him when he came downstairs, sitting at the table set with four places, with two of them filled. Seated with his mother was a round-faced woman whom he'd glimpsed at his mother's tea. Madeline was bustling in with a platter of meat and a steaming covered bowl, and his mother was speaking.

". . . and I said, 'Really, all these letters are the same these days, can't you give me any variation?' Oh, Richard, there you are—he's been playing with a new little friend, a French boy—Richard, Mrs. J thought she should look in on me and I said, 'Whatever for?' So I've asked her to stay for dinner."

"Most pleased to meet you," said Richard, making a slight bow. He dropped his head slightly toward his mother. After he found his chair, he stared down at the white plate before him, its edge ringed with a pattern of green leaves; and in its shiny center, like in a fairy story, he saw the face of the woman in the swing. Her longing eyes, the ribbons all undone beneath her chin. He glanced away. The steam was rising from the covered dish, and the round-faced woman was on the other side of it from him, half-obscured by the vapor.

F Jones must have known her, he thought.

". . . it's just that we'd missed you at cards," the round-faced woman was saying. "And your lovely stories."

F Jones must have known her to have painted her.

". . . the correspondence is just so . . . preoccupying. That's why I'm out of circulation. Just tell that to the others," his mother replied.

"Now, isn't there a lineage to that word that we ought to know," said the round-faced woman teasingly. She winked at Richard through the steam.

"Ah, yes, a lineage," said his mother in a light tone. Then suddenly: "The beef, how is the beef?"

"Tender and rare," said the woman. "Perfection. But the boy—the boy hasn't taken any."

"I'm not hungry," said Richard.

"Of course a boy's hungry," said the woman. "If he's been out playing."

"Out playing with a French boy," said his mother.

"All right," he said. He took a small piece, but he was careful not to put it on the shiny place on his plate that had been like some magic mirror, careful not to befoul that place with its blood when he cut it.

"Now, who is this French boy?" asked the round-faced woman.

From his mother, there was only the sound of her knife cutting through to click on china.

"Just some boy," said Richard. "Freddy. That's his name."

"Freddy?" said the round-faced woman.

"Frederick," said the boy, too sharply.

"Well, tell me about him," said the woman. Madeline was standing by the doorway, her eyes blank, waiting to remove plates or bring others.

"He's a boy like any other," said Richard.

"And his family?" asked the round-faced woman, smiling at him.

He glanced down at his plate, and then up at her again; the steam was gone; her face was full and red across the table from him.

"A regular family," said the boy. "Father, mother, and sister. No grandparents. No aunts or uncles. The four of them. They came here from France—from Brittany. He showed me a map. They stopped in Rome, then they came here. On a . . . ship. Across the waves." He closed his eyes for a moment. He saw the boats on the river, the waves they made. He opened his eyes, saw the folds of the tablecloth before him.

"Are you quite all right?" the woman asked.

He swallowed. "A piece of meat," he said. "Stuck." He pulled on the tablecloth, to straighten it.

"And what do his parents do?" asked the round-faced woman.

"I'm not sure about his mother," said Richard. And before he could stop it, it just slipped out. "His father is a painter."

"Should we discuss those we don't know?" said his mother with a quiet intensity.

It wasn't her words that made the boy gawk at her, for he had heard her say such things a hundred times or more. It was something else that made him look on her with wonder, and then shrink back, as if afraid. The round-faced woman couldn't see it, nor could Madeline. But he could. In the window's slanting light, he took in the shape of her cheekbones, the length of her nose, the roundness of her mouth, and thought that if you dressed her in blue and gave her a hat, if you took years away, if you undid the ribbons below her chin . . .

"Sorry," he said, catching their looks. "I was only repeating what Freddy told me. For all I know, he's not an artist at all."

~

The next morning the boy was sitting next to his tutor. Roskins, eye twitching, hair falling across his forehead, looked at him and then away. "Painting," he announced. "Like other arts, it represents man's paradoxical wish to create something false and believe in it as true. Sometimes it's more or less obviously false, a stage set whose works and pulleys we can glimpse."

"Like Impressionism," said the boy.

Roskins's eye grew still. "A fabricated scene made of dabs and bits of color—but for all that, it can exert a strange kind of enthrallment . . ." He shook his head; then he fumbled with several large books stacked on the table. A page dropped to the floor, and as he picked it up, he muttered, "Dutch painters"; then straightening, glanced at Richard and said, "You know you are the first boy who's ever asked for Netherlandish art."

"Of ships and seascapes," the boy added.

Roskins proceeded to open the book to various paintings, continuing to mumble to himself. He displayed prints of harbors and ships, and other scenes—landscapes, domestic scenes—as he flipped through the pages.

"Van Ruisdael," he said. "Here is a shore . . . and here, these little figures—wouldn't these be Netherlands hats?"

The boy shook his head.

"Dubbels," said Roskins. "*Yachts, Becalmed Near the Shore*. Cappelle, *A Dutch Yacht Firing a Salute*. Van de Velde the Younger, *Dutch Vessels, Close Inshore at Low Tide, and Men Bathing*. No hats there, I see. Wouwermans, *A View on a Seashore with Fishwives . . .*"

The prints flashed by, ships in harbors, boats off shore, reminding Richard of the one he'd envisioned, but none seeming quite right.

"No, no, no . . ." said Roskins, moving quickly past tranquil fields and orderly kitchens with bright and perfect fruit. "De Vlieger, *A Dutch Man-of-war and Various Vessels in a Breeze*. Is this quite what you wanted?"

The boy only shook his head, and kept his eyes focused on the pages.

"No, no, no," said Roskins, moving through a new set of portraits.

"Wait," said the boy. "Stop. Back—that one."

"It's not a Dutch ship," said Roskins crossly.

"Another page," said the boy. "There."

"Vermeer van Delft," Roskins was saying. "*Girl Interrupted at Her Music.*"

Oh, so nice to see you again.

And you, said the girl. *My, how you've grown.* She was a young, attractive woman with a kerchief over her head, staring out at him as if he—or the painter—had surprised her in the middle of her music lesson with a mustachioed gentleman.

How you used to look at me.

It was you—it was you I would see.

"Oil on canvas," Roskins was saying in a disinterested way. "Done around 1660. Says Vermeer could create the precision of still lifes, but with human subjects."

It was something like me. And you would laugh at the kerchief on my head.

"Let me see." Roskins was reading, his voice falling into the background like the clopping of horses, the swishing of fabric. "'Music-making was related to romance in the seventeenth century. The cupid in the background emphasizes the passionate relationship between the young woman and the mustachioed man, who are engaged in a music lesson, or perhaps a duet . . .'"

When I was little.

Once you put your shirt over your head, she said.

"I remember!"

"Master Richard . . ." Roskins was glaring at him. "How can you remember if I've just read this to you for the first time."

"I'm sorry," said the boy. "I was thinking of something else."

"Painting was your request. Now shall we get on to the ships."

"Wait."

Remember when you were picked up, your legs were kicking in the air, and you tried to touch the music book that was here with me. You tried to touch my face.

It was your face?

And he said you shouldn't do that, not to touch the paintings, the paintings were just to look at.

I remember! But who said that?

He did, silly. Remember . . .

And I said if you *can touch . . .*

Yes, you said if he could touch . . .

Yes.

And they laughed.

They?

Shadow went over her face, and the page turned. Roskins was again looking for ships.

"Wait," said the boy. "That painting. I've . . . well, I've seen it before."

Roskins flipped back, read a note, and smiled. "In a Netherlandish museum, no doubt. On one of your travels."

"I did see it."

"Maybe in a book."

"Not in a book," said the boy. "The actual painting." With the others, he wanted to add, but didn't say it. He must be mistaken. Unless he had traveled somewhere, to museums he didn't remember seeing, sailed to countries he didn't recall, unless he'd had some gypsy life before this that he couldn't remember, before this house he'd always known, that he was getting glimpses of like a pentimento.

He looked at the picture again, gazed deeply into her face where she sat at the table, sheaves of music in her hand. She was quiet now, just a figure. She was familiar, he could swear . . . Yet it wasn't quite the face he remembered—or perhaps it was. The blurred face of the woman in blue floated before his eyes. She could be everywhere now, when he looked, he could see her face everywhere: in the plate at dinner, in the face of his mother, shining through all the portraits as if she were underpainted.

". . . Jacob de Wet, the Elder," Roskins was saying, moving again through paintings of ships. "Vermeulen—well, it's an iced-over river. Van Ruisdael again . . ."

Later, when he accompanied Roskins to the door, he asked if he might keep some of the books, as he assumed they couldn't have gotten through them all. "Quite all right," said the man, and then with an edge of sarcasm to his voice: "We've only just scratched the surface."

~

He'd found a quicker way there, studying the guide to the city—a way that didn't require such a circuitous route. It was a clouded-over day, so different from the day F Jones had painted the woman in the swing, the woman he had to have known, who was now playing hide-and-seek with the boy in his nightmares and daydreams.

He simply had to see her again, in a place where she couldn't move away.

He was getting used to Hodge Lane: its narrow width, the way he had to get to the side when a horse and carriage made its way through, the shop with tobacco and pipes in the window, with a little figure of a man holding a tin of cigars. But he hardly glanced at that now, hardly paid attention to the mist that was filling the way; he was almost to the gallery, and even the sound of his steps on these stones felt familiar to him, like that of the walk of someone you knew.

He recognized too the tinkle of the bell, Madeline's mother sitting at her accustomed place in the far corner at the desk, another teacup in front of her, her hand running through her hair, Madeline just paces away from her, turning in a circle on one foot. He nodded to them, even though they didn't see him yet; he walked directly toward the wall where she would be hanging, taking a less circuitous route in here as well.

He thought it was the wrong wall at first, and he looked at the other paintings—the green bird, the horses—to orient himself. This too was somehow familiar, this looking around a room . . .

"Yes, she's gone," said Madeline, walking toward him with an expression that looked more eager than regretful. "Mummy's upset—and I am too. But it's not as if it was worth so very much. And at least it wasn't one of her favorites."

They'd hung another picture in the blank space where the portrait had been, a long and narrow painting of a tree that left too much of the wall between it and the others on either side.

"We called the police, and Mummy told them how I'd been telling everyone that was the monkey one, you know—they think maybe somebody pinched it because of that. For the curiosity value, they said. They said the lock on our door was really bad. But I don't think they really know anything."

He remained silent, still looking at the tree where her face should have been. He remembered a story that Roskins had once told him; he had even recited some verses about it: a myth of a beautiful young woman who had been changed into a laurel. The bark had covered her body, her neck, finally her face, until she had been lost forever. Strange how this new painting also was turning into an Impressionist work.

"You're crying!" Madeline said.

He gazed away from her, all around at the other pictures, up higher, to the windows above, and finally back to his shiny shoes. There were more scuffs on them now.

"It's just a picture," she said. "Or maybe things like this don't happen in France. Mummy, the French boy—he's . . ."

But he was walking away from her now. The bell tinkled—he was outside, where the light mist was falling. He started striding up Hodge Lane, when a figure caught up with him. Madeline again.

"I'm sorry," she said. "Mummy tells me I'm not polite enough—she says there's a column I should read that tells all about that kind of thing. So I'm to apologize, and to tell you this. Mummy knew—you liked that painting, and the other one by the painter, the one your aunt has. She's sorry your aunt can't come and buy this one now. And she said to tell you this. The other one, the R—"

"R Venus."

"Yes, the *R Venus,* she doesn't know what it means."

"It's a painting by someone named Velázquez. It's called *The Rokeby Venus*. It's almost naughty. I've seen it in the museum."

"Well, then, it won't matter."

"No, it won't."

She looked at him—her mouth seemed as if she were forcing it shut, when she wanted to open it and keep talking. And then, at last, she did, the words bursting from her, as all her words did.

"Just to tell you that the little *S* means a painting's been stolen."

"Well, that one couldn't be. I just saw it."

"I'm just telling you what she said. Oh, I don't care anyway."

She dashed off then, leaving the boy to look after her. The mist that was falling, and equally rising from the lane, made halos of every object. For a moment it was as if he were on a street of ghosts, and the lampposts, the awnings, even her figure, running from him, seemed doubled.

Chapter 14

He did not feel well for several days, but said nothing to his mother. He stayed alone, mostly in his room. Inside of him now there were all kinds of sensations: a heaviness in his chest that he thought of as a boulder, painted by Uccello; and—like in a Christian miracle by the Master of Werden—what seemed to be water streaming out of it in a waterfall. All day long, this water fell and fell, unseen, inside of him.

There were dimensions beyond dimensions inside of himself, walls opening to walls, pictures appearing to others.

The evening of the second day he took out the index card, and added the following:

B (Blue) Woman—F Jones (Stolen)
F (Farm) Life—F Jones (Stolen)
R (Rokeby) Venus—Velázquez (Stolen ?)
F (?) Jones—(Missing)

Then he wrote in the following lines:

Girl Interrupted at Her Music—Vermeer
? — ?
? — ?

because he knew there were others still to be found.

After a while, he picked up several of the art books that Roskins had let him borrow. Taking them from his bureau to his bed, he held them with their pages hanging loose beneath, and he slowly waved their covers along the creases in the spine, flapping them, as if they were birds coming in to roost on his bed. He laughed for a little while at the conceit, as any child might, before he turned them over and they were books again, with paintings inside.

Once again he started to look.

He turned the pages and saw scenes of windmills and skaters, landscapes giving out onto water. None of these were right. He turned another page.

There were ships in a harbor. Little men.

With Netherlands hats.

You found us!

They were speaking to him in a playful tone, those little men—a playful tone like children splashing water in a bath. They were rowing out, all still, away from the beach and bracken, out to the sailing ships lying in the calmed water, and even as his eyes misted over to see these familiar figures, he felt something else as well: that he wasn't sure he wanted to see them again.

Don't you remember how you used to look at us. Look at us and wonder if he was on our ship?

Oh, yes, said the boy. He paused. He had an urge to close the page, but instead, he asked: *Who was it I wondered about?* His eyes darted to the listing on the opposite page from the plate. *Dordrecht: Sunrise.* In a Netherlands museum. And the painter's name, which he said aloud, "Was it Aelbert Cuyp?"

Not him, silly.

I know, I . . .

It was the man with the mustache, they said. *You'd see him on the boat, on the little boat with her. And then later—*

Later?

After he'd gone. You'd come up and you'd talk to us, all us little men, as we rowed away on the calm sea and you'd wish he was with us, floating far, far away.

Yes, and she—

She would look down at you, she'd laugh and hold you in your blue suit, and then you'd say so she couldn't hear . . .

What would I say?

You'd say you hoped he never came back.

He looked away a moment. *I remember a boat on a still sea,* he said. *But that wasn't just your boat, was it? Not just this boat . . .*

What was it like? they asked.

He looked down, then back at them. *It had waves inside it. Waves that weren't . . . moving.*

You pretended it was a boat, you pretended they were waves, they said.

That boat was really something else, he said. *And the waves . . .* He closed his eyes. Thought of the school theatrical, the clothes flapping on the street. *The waves were cloth,* he said.

Yes, they said, *the waves were just cloth.*

He quietly closed the book, and a shadow poured over them and they were gone and sealed shut. All the little men on the boats. Quiet now.

He carried the books and put them back, no birds flying now. What would he have pretended was a boat? He didn't know. He couldn't know.

He went to his window and looked out—it was night. But

he could just see the dark blue of the leaves where they brushed the glass of his second-floor window, like the stubby fingers of a child.

~

His mother had to be out most of the day. A meeting with her editor. A very important conference, she said, smiling toward the kitchen doorway, then looking back and not meeting his eyes. She hadn't said anything about the boy taking his meals in his room, but now she said she was glad he was more himself, not good for one to stay too much in a room, and that was why she had to get out as well, didn't he see?

Yes, he was just beginning to see.

A carriage came for her mid-morning, its blinkered horse snorting and prancing as it waited. She walked quickly from the house, and let herself inside the carriage's dim interior, the door still closing as the coachman clicked the horse to a fast walk and the wheels began to turn.

Madeline was downstairs rustling in the kitchen when he reached for the doorknob, turned it, and despite the rushing voices, entered his mother's room. He had the same urge to back out, turn the page, close the book. But instead he went to her closet, located the painting of the farm—he was worried for a moment it had been further stolen. In addition to the same clippings in the box, there was a new one that detailed the successful theft of the painting at the Battersea Gallery. On a little assignment card with a pencil stub he wrote the name of the other gallery owner that was mentioned, *Ferguson,* in the block printing that Roskins was always trying to get him to move beyond.

He saw the same perfume bottles on top of her vanity, the vials of makeup she must have rarely used, as her face was regularly pale. For no reason at all he lifted up a little bottle of red, like a pot of paint. He glanced in her mirror as he held it in his hand, and was almost startled to see his face and not some other staring back. He put it down quickly, fumbling with it, almost breaking it.

He was glad to leave, even though he knew he wasn't quite finished. But this did seem like something he knew about, this going into places he shouldn't.

He nodded to Madeline, who was setting out his breakfast things in the dining room; then holding his breath, he walked into her drawing room as if it were the most natural thing, a polite visit, a tête-à-tête. Letters from her readers, mostly unopened, were stacked on the left side of her desk. On the right were only a few envelopes containing her responses. He picked one up and on the back flap read the familiar compact printing in which she'd written her return address:

Mrs. Abigail Foster
20 Church Walk

He replaced it with the others, feeling at a loss for what to do next. His glance fell to a large piece of foolscap with a good six inches torn from the top, the letter opener lying just below its neatly torn border. The light was glinting in through the window, and all at a loss for a moment he stared at the paper's watermark as if it were a caricature of him. But the impression left on the sheet below the part that had been torn away was clear enough for anyone to see—like forgotten figures showing through paint. He stared at the indented letters, these shadows of the words and numbers she had written and removed:

TCA
25 Wentworth

It would have to be the initials and address of her editor. But, once again with that odd hesitation and no more than a fool's comprehension of why he was doing it, he blocked them out on his little card with the stub of pencil.

When he glanced back at her desk from the door, the sun catching the letter opener made it glow like molten silver.

As he walked into the dining room, he saw Madeline sitting at the table. He was fingering the card in his pocket, and he didn't feel at all himself: He felt he was not walking exactly on the ground, but over some precipice, out on thin air. Madeline was sitting with her head in her hands, seemingly deep in thought. She could be a portrait, of course. And seeing her there, he felt for a moment a comfort that perhaps none of this was real, and that the jottings on the card he held were like the strange code of the tramps: intricate, yet something he would never understand.

Late morning, he was on the omnibus, rocking to its motion, following his finger along the map opened in his lap. He knew where to get out, how to walk toward the door through the passengers, which way to turn, which street to take. Once in the museum, he remembered some of the gallery rooms he'd visited, and he wanted to return to visit those he was thinking of as his friends: the young man playing skittles, the saint looking at the crucifix appearing on the deer, even the sad woman with the opened letter weeping before the pool.

Hello, they'd say, *Oh, hello,* and *So good to see you again,* and *Where have you been a-roaming?*

He didn't linger in any of these familiar places. He walked through the museum as he had sat on the bus, as if the paintings flashing by were sights outside the windows that he was merely passing.

He was heading to one painting in particular, which Madeline had said was stolen. *R Venus*. If it somehow wasn't there, at least he would know he was right about something—at least he could count on the predictability of absence.

He was starting to believe that he was somehow strangely responsible for the thefts. There was something in his looking at these paintings that made them disappear; it wouldn't surprise him if there was an outbreak of losses in Netherlands museums. He realized then that his walking straight ahead and not looking at the canvases that lined the walls on either side of him was out of that belief, that his very eyes would cause them to turn missing, maybe burn them up like intensified rays of the sun. But as frightening as this thought was, he also knew it wasn't true. It was, after all, just a distraction against what he suspected from the clippings of the thefts, from the absence on the gallery wall: that there was someone else out there, besides him and his mother, someone else wandering through the same imaginary gallery that he was trying to map. And this someone was ripping the paintings off its walls.

He passed a guard and lowered his head. In the quiet

gallery where it had hung, without looking up, he counted off the paintings until he stood before it. When he did gaze up, he couldn't believe at first that it was gone, replaced by a Madonna and child, bathed in radiant light. Gone, like she was gone. He looked wildly around him, and then back. How could someone have lifted it from here? And how could Madeline have known?

He felt frightened, but he made himself slow down. He made himself walk, until he reached the guard again.

"Excuse me," the boy said. "I'm sorry. That painting."

"Yes, which?"

"Velázquez. *The Rokeby Venus*."

"Yes."

"I'm sorry, it's been stolen," he said. He realized one of his own eyes was twitching.

The guard looked quickly to the wall, and then back to the boy, his mouth slightly upturned in amusement.

"Moved."

"Moved?"

The guard nodded his head to his left, as the boy rapidly turned. On the facing wall he saw it.

"Oh, yes, moved. Quite sorry."

His heart was pounding as he approached it. He looked at the tag, as if for confirmation. He gazed up into the painting, tilting his head. A woman after her bath, reclining on a couch, the only view of her face a reflection, where an angel was holding a mirror.

R Venus.

There were other visitors in the room, talking and

exclaiming about the works, and they distracted him. He stared up, willing them to silence, and then the angel spoke.

They'll be coming by any moment, so I'll tell you. She did like to look in her mirror, she did like to look. As did you. And you would stand by her, and look at her, and then look at her reflection in the mirror.

I would look at her, and then at her reflection.

Something dimly registered in his mind then, about the painting being marked stolen, while it was still there in front of him.

Yes, you'd look at her. And then later, when the door was closed, you'd look at me holding the mirror, and her face there.

The Venus's face.

The Venus's face, said the angel.

My face, said the woman.

I'm not sure it was your face, said the boy. He dropped his head, and after a moment, looked up at them again. He couldn't be sure.

The people were making their way around the perimeter of the room, commenting on color and light, and the boy turned and watched them, thinking of how paintings felt, being so helplessly stared at, so cruelly compared to others.

He looked back to the angel.

They're coming, said the angel, *so I'll tell you quickly. You did move then, you moved your hand up and down, standing by her in the mirror.*

Yes, I remember, I was painting—

You pretended you were painting. And he—

He? The one I wished away on the boat?

Yes.

But who was he? the boy asked. *The man with the mustache?*

Yes, the walrus mustache. And sometimes he liked it when you would paint her.

Yes, I remember that.

And she liked it too, and all of you would laugh.

Yes . . .

And sometimes he didn't, he didn't want you to touch.

Oh . . .

And then they would close the door, and that's when you would come and talk to me.

I remember now, when they would close the door. But I would come all the way here?

You would come and talk to me, and her face in the mirror.

It was her face? And what would I say?

You'd say if he can touch . . .

The people were two paintings away; they were saying the face of the Madonna before them was not as beatific as the one in the other gallery, and that the face of the child she was holding looked like the wise and shrunken face of a man.

What else? said the boy, urgently now, there wasn't much time. *What else did I say, what . . . what else did I see?*

You saw the harbor, and you saw the little boys with horns.

The little boys. Yes, in a field. And I used to wonder, did I have horns too? One had a helmet . . .

Yes, one had his helmet.

The people, two women and a man, had come upon him now, were standing behind him.

"Velázquez," said one of the women.

"Oh, yes," said the man. "He was a master."

The painting was growing flat before the boy, turning into just oils on canvas.

He heard one of the women whisper to the others, and the hair on the back of his neck stood up, when he heard her say the word "boy."

"Yes," said the other woman, and more whispers. The words "proper . . . not proper . . . just a boy," and the man saying, ". . . can hardly see the harm in it, it's just her backside." The boy thought how they must be looking at him, but they didn't know he was eavesdropping on them. The other woman said, "Yes . . . but nude . . . impressionable . . . a boy's imagination . . ." and he took a step forward, their whispers fading into the sound of shoes sliding across the floor, into the sound of other people's voices hushing and shushing through the great and silent rooms. And then the painting changed: There was a glow to it, and dimension. The angel spoke to him again.

And sometimes you begged he'd go away on her ship.

Her ship?

And ever so slowly he saw it: the low couch she was lying on. The narrow bed with its loose and wrinkled covers, depending on how old you were when you viewed it, could look very much like a little ship.

Chapter 15

When he first heard the knock at the front door, he thought it was Roskins, coming back for the book. He'd returned the rest to his tutor, asking just to keep the one that contained the paintings he thought he'd recognized. He'd added to the card:

Girl Interrupted at Her Music—Vermeer
Dordrecht: Sunrise—Aelbert Cuyp

It wasn't Roskins who was knocking. As the boy backed away from the door, his heart pounding—backed away without being seen, he thought—he kept his eye on the figure outside. It was a man who had thick sideburns, and a large belly that protruded beneath his brocaded vest, and as the man knocked again, and waited, and then knocked yet again, a face that was growing increasingly grim, as the boy could see through the crack in the curtains where he'd stationed himself.

He didn't like answering the door, especially to strangers; his mother had said disreputable men could sometimes knock on a person's door, knock and pass over the threshold, perhaps like that hobo he had seen. Although he knew he was too old to hide, he'd partially wrapped himself in the curtains as a compromise between staying and leaving.

It struck him then that this man could be the painter F Jones; perhaps he had come to see how his work *Farm Life* was displayed, to see if it was adequately protected from whoever was trying to take his paintings from their rightful places. Roskins had told him something about the valuation of paintings: Some that seemed worth very little during the painter's life could become worth many, many times more after his death; or unknown artists could sometimes go quickly into demand, and the prices for their works soar. And paintings that became especially valuable could even be counterfeited. Perhaps something like this had happened to F Jones, or was about to happen to him, and someone was out there taking them to some foreign market. Roskins had said something about foreign markets, and the boy knew that Madeline's uncle was in Germany, buying paintings.

All this ran through his head as he twirled and untwirled himself in the curtain, over the intermittent knocking of the man. When he looked again, he saw the man turning to go and the French Madeline approaching the door. She must have heard the knocking all the way in the kitchen. She shot the boy an odd look as she pulled the door open, and bursting into the house came the man's agitated voice.

"Well, I must say—I was thinking someone was home and then almost gave up. It wasn't *polite* of me, I suppose—to knock so long and so loud. Not polite—but is she in?"

Madeline held the door open; she tilted her head slightly, but didn't respond verbally—as the boy expected she wouldn't—in this alien tongue.

"I say," the man began again, and Richard was torn between watching what unfolded and coming out himself. The man's face had grown grim again, and Richard could see first him and now the growing red on Madeline's cheek.

"I say, is Mrs. Foster in?"

Richard now realized that by only slightly shifting his gaze, a third view was afforded to him. He could just make out his mother's arm and part of her head through the doorway, where by the looks of it she was sitting quite still in the drawing room. Although the voices must have carried that far, his mother gave no sign that she heard, or that the speaking of her name had an impact, other than causing her to raise her hand briefly to the visible part of her forehead and brush aside a strand of hair. Except for the man's exasperated voice, it was a dumb show he was watching, almost entertaining in its own way. The man shaking his head; Madeline blushing, her fingers white on the door; his mother taking down the letter opener from a stack of correspondence and then putting it back.

The spell of this—of him watching, of these three separate bodies in space, all having something to do with one another—was broken when Madeline turned abruptly to him and said, *"Venez ici, Richard,"* none too gently. Almost in slow motion he unwound himself from the folds of the curtain and walked toward the door.

"Venez vite!"

"You speak English?" the man asked him as he came into sight.

The man was taller than he appeared from the window. The comic aspects of his bluster were no longer present, as the veins stuck out in his neck when he asked his questions in a tight voice. Richard stepped back, out of the doorway's rectangle of light, and then was pushed into it again by Madeline's firm fingers on his back.

Richard only nodded in response, as if to recapture the mute distance of the scene.

"Well, if you do, or you don't, will you give Mrs. Foster this? Please," he added, which made a cord in his neck stick out.

He handed forth a card; it was shaking slightly in his fingers.

"And if you understand me, tell her we need to hear from her. We can't leave space—we have a newspaper to run." He broke off, and wiped his mouth where some spittle had formed on the inside of his lips. Richard stepped back again. "I'm trying to say—we can't leave space for her column if we don't hear from her."

Richard looked at Madeline for help, but she was now in the role of the mute observer. His eyes shifted to a place on the man's brocaded vest, the pattern of black on gold, like bloodshot in an eye. "I do think it's all right," said Richard quietly. "She told me. She was yesterday meeting with her editor."

"I am her bloody editor," said the man.

Richard looked down at the card in his hand.

Richard Borchard
Editorial Department

These were not the initials TCA; the address printed was not 25 Wentworth. And this man, as if echoing the boy's own confusion, was looking from him to Madeline and back, perhaps trying to find adequate comprehension from the two that he was unable to find in one. "Just tell her—tell her, blast it, that I'm trying to be polite about it. On my end. But she needs to hold up hers."

The man turned abruptly and walked away. Richard started when he felt Madeline's hand on his arm, holding it still, while she examined the card in his hand. Their eyes met, and almost at the same moment, broke as they turned and looked back into the house, at the woman seated so still before her table.

"I shall give her the card," said Richard.

He quietly tapped on the door frame and then entered her room, hardly thinking that it was a rule that he was breaking. That rule—other rules—seemed like part of a life that had become lost.

He laid the card before her on the table.

"Oh, yes," she said. "Thank you."

"He was just here," said Richard.

"Yes. Thank you." She faintly smiled, and then, as if he had gone, or become still himself, she blankly continued her staring out. When he was about to turn, his eye was caught by the card where she had placed it. The little square card. Her face framed by her hair and hand. He was reminded of the little plaques in the museum next to the oils, and yes, he could see it. His mother was turning into a painting.

But as he continued to gaze on her, this illusion would not hold. He saw her in all her three dimensions: There was a heart in her, and fine blue veins of her blood beneath pale skin, and trembling eyelids and breath inside she could hardly keep in, that made her nostrils ever so slightly flare. Maybe she had always been this way; maybe he had only lately let himself know it. There was massive disarray behind the polite and composed portrait she tried to present: Within her, there were rooms beyond rooms of dark and light, clashing images of angels and fiends, saints and beasts, and tempests at sea.

~

A light rain was falling the next day. It wasn't often that rain was depicted in paintings, but here it was now, and he and Madeline took their umbrellas from the stand in the hall and set out down the walk.

Madeline had needed to do the shopping and Richard had told his mother he wished to accompany her. She hadn't objected, as he thought she wouldn't. It had been difficult at first to make Madeline understand what he wanted. He'd had to use the glossary in the back of *La Carte et le Guide de la Cité,* and even that wasn't enough; so he'd pantomimed some and she had finally gotten a more complete English-*Français* dictionary from her little room off the kitchen, and by stringing together several nouns with pidgin spoken verbs, he'd made her understand where they were going and what he wanted from her when they got there—at least he thought he had.

There were others on the street, some with umbrellas, some squinting under hats and caps. *"La parapluie,"* Madeline had said, and he had replied, "Umbrella." It could almost seem they were just out for a friendly walk in the rain, especially when she put her hand on his arm, this girl at least four years older than he, a big sister she could be, a cousin from the Continent, pointing out as she did the fence, *la enceinte,* and the shop window, *fenêtre de magasin*. He had indicated how the fence post that had been knocked awry had been replaced by a new one—he gestured as he tried to explain this to her, and he felt such a surge of joy as he did so. She laughed as he swung his arm in a particularly wide arc, and for a moment he felt too wound up, like some reckless toy that might go marching off a tabletop.

They walked on. But his spirits didn't dampen. Above a break in the sky there were clouds that reminded him of Titian or Rafael; and this woman walking toward them, hunched over, with her white peaked cap, could have stepped out of a painting by the Netherlands painter Vermeer. He thought how he'd like to be able to explain this to her, this third vocabulary he was learning.

They passed a school.

"L'école," said Madeline. Her face turned thoughtful as they looked up into the windows, where students were in rows, in their ties and jackets, one carrying a paper toward the front of the room. *"Comment vous n'êtes pas* . . . in the school?"

"How come—how come I don't go to school?"

"Oui, oui."

He laughed for getting it right, but his flush of pride subsided as he thought about her words.

"Roskins," he said. "I have Roskins."

"Pourquoi?"

"Because," he said. But he felt all at a loss—a memory of the time he'd been in school rising and fading, fading to nothing as he looked up through the windows. The instructor was lacing his fingers together as he addressed his pupils. They seemed orderly—all in their rows. It reminded him of when he had walked to the river, and seen the ships and the waves. It wasn't any of that which had really frightened him. So perhaps it hadn't been the school either.

She was searching his face, and as if she could sense his distress, she simply shrugged and applied pressure to his hand to move on.

The opening in the sky above them had closed, and the rain seemed to be falling harder now—or maybe he just noticed it more from their standing still.

"Umbrella," he said. *"Parapluie,"* and he raised and lowered it and gave a tight little smile. Then they turned into Hodge Lane.

They walked past Number 10; from the far side of the street he looked searchingly in the window. The other Madeline wasn't anywhere to be seen. He had the funny thought that they were the same person, got up in different guises, and he looked over at the young woman beside him as if to reassure himself it wasn't so. Then he gazed back into the gallery. As he had anticipated, the portrait of the woman in blue had not been returned.

Now he saw Madeline's mother. She was just approaching the shop from the opposite way, making ready to unlock it. She could have been anywhere, the boy reasoned, out to get some tea or biscuits. But it wasn't lost on him that she had come from the direction of their own destination.

They walked on, and he didn't think they'd been seen.

Ferguson's, the name of the other gallery he'd copied on the note card, was around the corner from Hodge Lane, at 15 Montrose Walk. As they entered, he could see at once it was a finer sort of gallery. There were no bits of plaster peeling, no teacup stains. On the walls were framed bunches of fruit, some horses in a field, an Impressionist view of a riverbank. He didn't know precisely the artist's hand—he'd only seen the two paintings in such different styles—but he thought that if any of his others should be there, they might stand out with a kind of glow that he would immediately recognize. A young man in a striped waistcoat was sitting at the far end of the long room beside a little table, where there were note cards in a metal holder. After a moment, he rose and walked up to the boy and Madeline. The young man bent slightly from the waist as he asked if he could help them, and Madeline declined, politely, in French, as they had agreed.

The plan was simple enough. It would be a kind of masquerade, in which he and Madeline assumed roles slightly different from their own: Madeline was to be his cousin from the Continent, and, as at the Battersea Gallery, he was to be there on behalf of his aunt, who lived in England and France. His uncle had been lost at sea, in a channel crossing. They would look around the gallery with an air of connoisseurs. After Madeline declined any help, they would look over some of the paintings, and then after they'd considered and discussed and shaken their heads, Madeline would ask for any paintings by a particular artist, *un Monsieur F Jones,* and then the young master would chime in that yes, his aunt, who lived in both France and England, liked his work quite well—it had been a favorite of his late uncle's—and she was relying on the two of them to make acquisitions.

But, unfortunately to the boy's way of thinking, the clerk didn't politely withdraw; instead, he said: *"Je parle un peu de Français."*

"C'est vrai?"

"Yes, a little, *un peu*. I've completed my . . . that is, *J'ai fais mes études à l'université*."

Madeline shook her head. *"Je n'ai jamais étudié à l'université, mais . . ."* Here she blushed and the young man laughed.

"For all that, I'm just a clerk in my uncle's gallery," he answered, straightening his cravat in his collar. "But if you wanted to study—in a university—I'm sure you'd be able to," he added flatteringly.

"J'espère que oui."

All of this was said rapidly above the boy's head. He shot a remonstrative look toward Madeline, as if to say, *Remember who we said we'd be.*

But the young man was going on. "Although it's not a bad thing to be in trade. I'm grateful to my uncle for it, don't misunderstand."

She was supposed to politely decline and then they'd look at the pictures on the walls . . .

"And who's he?" asked the clerk, nodding toward Richard but addressing Madeline.

"Mon frère," said Madeline. My brother.

"We're cousins," said the boy at the same time.

"Well, which is it?" said the young man, laughing. Madeline, realizing her mistake, brought her hand to her mouth. It was all she could do not to titter.

"Well, no matter," said the man, again addressing Madeline. "I love the chance to use my French again. Wait—how's this: *Je ne pensais pas que je die encore l'occasion de parler Francais aussi.*"

"Bon. Et pour moi—how do you say, a chance to . . . repeat my English?"

The clerk laughed—he *was* just a clerk.

"What about the boy, whoever he is? Don't you practice with him?"

Richard could sense her shift, and she leaned forward toward the man. *"Il est un enfant trop tranquille et sérieux."*

"Well, that's no fun," the clerk said, staying in this close posture with her.

"She's just a cook," said Richard.

"I'm sorry," said the young man, drawing slightly away from her.

"We're not related at all. She cooks for me."

"Well." He looked from one to the other, at a loss.

Richard again spoke. "But that's not important. *Pas important.*" Why he'd wanted to assume these guises in the first place was lost to him. "We are simply . . . *nous sommes* . . . looking for work by, paintings by . . ." He looked to Madeline; it might still have greater weight if it didn't come from a boy, but she was looking away from him. "Work by . . . *les peintures comme . . . Monsieur F Jones.*"

"Come again?" It was all the clerk could do not to laugh at his halting, awkward speech, Richard could see that. But it was worse than that: Madeline too was suddenly red-faced, her hand over her mouth. The boy looked from her to a painting on the wall behind her, a river going out to a gray sea. Coldly, as cold as that sea, he looked back to her.

Now she seemed to remember some part of her assumed role in his little charade.

"Oh, oui. Le Monsieur F Jones. Un artiste commendable. Avez-vous des peintures de Monsieur F Jones?"

"She means Mr. F Jones," said the boy. "My uncle's English and French—and my aunt's drowned." He'd gotten it wrong, but he continued: "And she collects his work."

The young man looked from one to the other as if they were both daft, but when he heard Richard pronounce the name of the artist in an understandable way, he shrugged. He led them to the table and pulled open a ledger.

"Jones, Jones . . ." said the clerk, flipping the pages. He glanced up once at Madeline and grinned. Despite that, on seeing the book, the boy felt that it still might work. If the paintings here that had been stolen had been by him—if they were at least among those paintings—it would give him a link. He so badly wanted a map, a link . . .

Madeline was blushing again, her hand at her mouth.

The clerk, while looking, was making a comic face. He seemed not at all bounded by a sense of propriety. And Madeline was trying—she was trying not to laugh.

The boy looked down. Coming off his cheek he could taste little drops of salt water, sweat or tears of frustration, he couldn't tell which.

And so it all seemed Impressionist when the clerk said, "Well, sorry." His face was a blur, as if it were linked to the woman in blue. "We did have some, but, hello—they've been misplaced."

"Stolen," murmured the boy.

"Well, yes." He gave Richard an odd look. "*Mars and Venus* was one," the clerk went on. "I do remember that one," he said, more serious now, as if Richard's guessing right about them being stolen had given him some weight. The clerk looked at Madeline and cleared his throat. He seemed nervous, perhaps embarrassed. "There was . . . well, a real scene in the middle of it. In a field. And all around the edges, these little putti."

"*Putti?*" asked Madeline.

"These little cherubs—boys with horns."

You saw the little boys with horns . . .

It suddenly didn't matter if their masks had fallen down, if she had blushed or laughed.

"I should like to see," said Richard.

The clerk hesitated a moment, shrugged, and then swung the ledger around. The print on the page was hard to read, webbed and unblotted. *Mars and Venus*.

"By F Jones," said the boy.

"By F Jones," said the clerk. He turned the ledger back around and then picked up a square of paper clipped to the bottom of the page. "Hello," he said as he read it. "Someone else has been by about it." The boy could see that *Battersea Gallery/10 Hodge Lane* was embossed at the top of the card, with inked-in writing below it that he couldn't decipher.

The clerk looked up from the ledger to the two of them; the mood between them all had shifted and grown serious. "Now maybe you can help me out," he said. "Why are people looking for this second-rate copyist?"

Chapter 16

He left Madeline at a busy corner, standing for a moment and watching her disappear into the crowds, into all the anonymous cloaks and dresses. She'd kept her distance from him during this walk; he understood that the rude way he'd punctured their pretended relationship before the clerk had made everything momentarily different between them.

He pulled the note card from his pocket and flipped it over, from *Ferguson* to *TCA/25 Wentworth,* the address his mother had written out when she'd said she was visiting her editor. He stood in a doorway and consulted *La Carte et le Guide* until he found an avenue and a street by that name.

As the avenue was nearer, he started with it: a long and narrow brick-covered way of attached houses, piano music coming from one. There were no newspaper offices, hardly any shops. If she had visited a rival paper, it hadn't been here. He walked toward the end of the street, the numbers descending and finally ending in number 30. There was not even a 25.

He arrived at the other street about half an hour later. He was hungry; but with what he still had to find, he wouldn't be able to go immediately back home. He purchased a roll from a vendor's cart, and stood chewing it by a bench on a square.

He threw out the rest of the roll and started walking. It grew more chilly as the numbers descended; he heard birds crying, glimpsed them circling. He turned from a shabby row of houses and saw he was near the river again, in a different part. Wentworth continued in a curving lane, with bricks missing in what seemed the street's version of the rotting teeth of those who were laughing and talking loudly on its corners.

There was some kind of shop with scraps of iron in its little front yard; a couple of tumble-down dwellings; a shack surrounded by boats in various states of disrepair. He passed these, certain it was the wrong street. His mother would never come here; he must have miscopied it. He began to feel more and more uncomfortable as he walked, and was met by stares. A young man in a worn top hat walked for a while by his side, saying he must be new to the neighborhood and tipping his hat in an oddly friendly manner. He soon dropped away in the face of Richard's unresponsiveness. Richard passed another dwelling, with a broken front window. In front of an empty storefront, lying in the weeds, was a sign that said *Pleasure Cruises*.

He walked up to the building and stared into it for a moment, through the clouded glass.

Up and down the street, numbers were missing; he saw nothing with the initials he'd copied, which after all, might be a person's initials.

A shout came up ahead of him, and he turned toward it. Two men were speaking loudly to each other. They were dressed as seamen, and others behind them had grouped together on the steps of a pub, standing before its open door as the argument grew in intensity. Despite all the ruckus below, the boy liked the look of the sign: a man's face with a patch over one eye, in a blue sailor's uniform. *Corporal's Arms,* it said, in red paint.

He wondered if his father had been a corporal when he had died in the wreck of that ship from which his mother had been saved. The ship, *The Diana* . . . But this story of his father seemed suddenly thin and pale in the reality before him, an unconvincing sticker pasted over something much deeper and more obscure.

There was another shout. One of the men who'd been arguing was clearly drunk and could hardly stand; he took a swing at his opponent that nearly carried him around in a kind of corkscrew. He had to take several short, quick steps to regain his balance, and jeers and laughter came from the crowd. With nothing approaching a real fight, the spectators began to disperse. Richard watched as one of the onlookers left the steps, carrying a bottle, heading back up the shabby lane. Dressed in a pea coat, he was walking in an unusual manner, in a kind of rolling gait, and even from some distance the boy could see his brightly polished, almost shining boots.

Watching the man now, the boy was momentarily back in the kitchen; Madeline was in front of him, the hobo was walking away after delivering his strange message to his mother, which could have been the raving of a madman.

Tell her that Mr. B—Mr. B is back.

Even if it seemed the same man, his mother couldn't

know such a man as this. And he wouldn't be able to come to their door in their respectable neighborhood. He'd stand out; people would wonder, gossip.

Unless he was in the guise of a tramp.

The remaining stragglers walked inside; the door slammed.

Number 25.

He shot a look at the sign—the eye patch there as if someone were wearing a blinder, only half-seeing.

Corporal's Arms.

He stared at the card, and wished he were wrong about it. But it was quite clear. The initials, TCA, would match. He just had to add the word *the*—as one might do who was in the habit of being polite.

~

An hour later, he was standing before the Uccello painting of the battle, in an almost empty gallery room. And then—he was within it.

He walked among the knights again, waving his hand and speaking loudly to all those surrounding: *I could have run after the man. Or better, I could have gone in, into that pub, and said, Is there a Mr. B here, please, is there a Mr. B here? I could have asked that, because that was who he talked about, the fellow with the odd walk. But I didn't like those men.*

He made a few feints at a knight on a gray charger who had a battle-ax raised.

If any of them had given me trouble, I would have gone like this— He waved his hand wildly, in some combination of a stabbing and slashing motion. *But I just didn't want to. Even*

St. George wouldn't have wanted to. He sat down next to a fallen knight, who was drastically foreshortened so that he was not much larger than a child.

If my mother had been in there, I would have gone in. If she had been in . . . He stopped a moment. *If she had been in some kind of trouble . . .*

He was striding across the museum floor now, walking quickly from the painting, gasping for breath, and he didn't know why.

He strode past paintings he recognized, and some that were strangers. By the look of it, as he went from gallery to gallery, he was moving in some miraculous manner forward and backward in time, past earlier paintings in a simpler, Romanesque style—holy men and women with thick gold halos around their heads like dinner plates—and then forward through the years to a slightly Impressionistic street where women in black were holding umbrellas, and one especially was looking at him with such yearning in her eyes as she held an empty basket. But he couldn't stop, he couldn't stand for very long in front of any of them, no, he really couldn't stay.

He had to find the putti, the little boys with horns, in the painting called *Venus and Mars.*

Why are you looking for it if it's stolen? cried out a woman standing before a pianoforte.

Yes, the man at the gallery said it's been stolen, said a distinguished gentleman on an opposite wall, with a large dog standing by his side.

He ended up in an area given to Netherlands paintings:

Those were the ones that F Jones seemed to have liked. He scanned the serene beaches, the landscapes dotted with windmills, the decorative rooms narrowing and vanishing.

He closed his eyes, made himself think; he called on all the afternoons he'd spent with Roskins.

Mars and Venus. They were originally Greek deities. And the Romans . . . the Romans had copied from the Greeks: They had taken their gods, called them different names.

He headed to the Italian paintings.

There were sumptuous Madonnas and transfigured saints, the savior rising from his tomb in radiant light. He read the names of the artists as he passed them: Titian, Michelangelo, Montegna, Crevali.

And then he saw them—on the far wall.

Here we are, here!

He slowed, almost stopped. He had an urge to go back the way he'd come. Delaying, he read aloud the names of the painters he passed as he made his way toward them, the canvases all halos and golden light. He felt their syllables in his mouth and on his lips—Georgione, Raphael, Corregio—as if he were just learning to speak.

And finally: B . . . B . . . Botticelli.

He was close to them, and he could see the little boys clearly now, clambering over the field. One was wearing the helmet of the warrior Mars, while others carried his lance and peered over it as if they were peeking over the sideboard of a bed.

I knew, he said. *I knew you weren't stolen.*

Not from here, said the little boys.

Yes, not from here. That's what I thought, said the boy. *Because you're not by F Jones.*

Not by the second-rate copyist, said the little boys. *You know that now. And you know something else.*

What?

The unforeseen consequences.

He stood there a moment, his breath coming out hard. *Mars and Venus,* he finally said.

Battles and weddings, said the little boys, in high voices like babies.

I do remember you, he said.

And we remember you. From nine years ago, we remember you.

He stared up at them, like a small child at an adult. He saw that another of them was crawling through the breastplate of the god Mars. They were making off with the arms of the fallen warrior.

You don't want to look, they said.

I am looking at you, he said.

No, you don't want to, they said.

I don't know what you mean.

At Mars and Venus, they said. *At the two of them. Don't you see—right before you?*

As if a screen were lifted, he saw what they were talking about; a hole opened in his stomach, and his breath grew short again. That he had known the painting was here, that there were two sets of paintings with the same name, now seemed unimportant compared to what he had really missed. For he had looked all around the outside of the picture, but not at its central subject, which he now saw: the woman and the man, the maiden and the warrior. Venus and Mars.

She was lounging on the ground, propped on one elbow, wearing only her nightdress with its golden border that was a magical continuation of her hair. She was looking across the languorous length of her body at the man opposite, who was mostly nude except for a cloth around his waist. The man was asleep, his head thrown back. He appeared a warrior defeated but yet dreaming of the pleasure of his defeat. And the little boys were all around them, carrying off his lance, his helmet, crawling through his breastplate. They were looking at the couple, leering at them, at the man and woman lying on the field of grass as if on a bed.

Or on a ship.

He said to the putti, *Were you in the room?*

We weren't there, and then we were.

Her room.

Yes.

He gave it to her.

Yes, you remember that. You saw him working on it, and it wasn't there, and then it slowly came out of nowhere and it was—the colors and figures and us! And then you made the little figures on the paper, with the brush and with your fingers. And you gave it to her.

Yes, I made it with my box of paints. She liked it.

She laughed and he laughed.

Yes, I remember, Richard said.

And then you looked at us. And she didn't think it was good, she said you shouldn't.

But I saw you there.

Sometimes they didn't know you were there. But we saw you—you would look at us.

I would look at your eyes. Just at your eyes.

And then you would say, if he *can look . . .*

Yes, that's what I said.

And one time in the room he saw you, he laughed and his mustache blew out from his mouth, and he said to her, the boy's looking.

And her face—her face looked sad.

And he laughed and said, don't worry, he doesn't understand. And she said, you shouldn't have made her face that way. If she ever—

She?

And he said, she won't, she won't. She'd never expect. And then he said, there there, now. He said cooo cooo cooo. He said la, she said la la laaaa.

Richard looked away as the little boys grew silent. When he looked up again, he saw something else that he had not seen before. The man in the gallery had been wrong: These were not cherubs, not boys, not putti. They had the faces of infants, but they had not only the horns he remembered but had furry, thick legs with hooves—the legs of goats, of rams. Powerful legs that could propel them quickly, wildly, to chase or run. These were not innocent children: They were infant satyrs—or they were now. Perhaps they had been children, but when they came upon the couple lying in the field, they had in that moment grown the horns and thickened legs of beasts.

~

It was cold outside the museum, and it felt strange to be there. People were walking this way and that, carrying on their normal lives. He could almost believe that he could walk among them, as one of them—that there was no danger here. But he still didn't quite believe it. Just as he didn't quite disbelieve that he really could go into that half-world of paintings, where figures spoke to him, and he spoke to them.

There was something more they needed to tell.

He walked through the gathering darkness, down the lane where he lived, through the open gate. His mother came out of the drawing room just as he entered: She must have heard his feet on the stones of the walk. He stood there, still, bracing for something, perhaps for her to strike him again; but she was smiling, a thin smile like a ticket pasted over something deeper, and her pulse was throbbing in her throat.

"Please," she said, reading from a piece of paper. "A function word to allow the speaker to be polite in addressing another." She glanced up. "It derives from the Latin root *placere,* to be pleasing. Pleasure, you see. And most interesting, before that, the Greek, *plax*—flat surface. Related to placid." She looked at him, still smiling, the way a gentlewoman should comport herself even in extremity. "And that is what many of my readers seem not to understand. Pleasure—a placid surface. An unroiled surface. Yet they seem to find pleasure in turbulence. And then they write to me. Make it smooth again, they say." Her voice caught. "Make it flat."

"Yes," said the boy. Across the gulf between them, her eyes seemed to catch the remorse in his. "Please," he said.

She shook her head and looked down, as if willing herself into stillness. When she spoke, her voice was filled with warmth. And a deep sorrow. "If only I could," she said.

Chapter 17

He couldn't sleep that night. He lay in his sheets, winding and unwinding. When he went to his door, he heard his mother writing, the familiar sound of scratching coming from the drawing room. She must be catching up on her correspondence—for unanswered correspondence is like a friend you have wronged. The sound was familiar, but different. It sounded quicker, rustling like animals running through dried leaves. There were so many different kinds—lizards and spiders, insects and mice. That was how he pictured it.

He went back and sat on his bed, lit the lantern on his table, and in its flickering light he drew out the card and added:

Mars and Venus—F Jones; (Stolen)

He'd seen the one in the museum, but the other had been taken from the gallery. He didn't know where it had gone, or who exactly had taken it. But he did know now—as he had understood for certain in the museum when he found it—that there were two sets of paintings: the originals in the museums and the others that were in the galleries he'd been to and perhaps in galleries he hadn't. Maybe this was something that was obvious, something he should have understood earlier; if that was so, why hadn't he? He shook his head. And there was more he didn't like to think about: that he was in here lining them up on a note card, and someone was out there lining them up in some other way, for some other purpose.

Just like there was Madeline here, and Madeline there, and his mother downstairs, and . . .

He could hear her scratching from the room below, the envelopes tearing and falling, the strange frightened animals running from the forest fire, scampering before the flood. It was simple; it was quite straightforward. If he looked at his mother in a certain way; if he imagined years taken from her, and her wearing a blue dress, and a wide hat on her head, with its ribbons undone . . .

He went back to what he understood. There were paintings in the museums, and the reproductions in the galleries, that had once been somewhere else. In a room. And someone was stealing the paintings. Someone was stealing them all. That was all there was to it.

He looked around his room as his logic seemed to break, and a deep swell rose from his chest and heart and threatened to drown him. In his mind's eye, the figures in the paintings were no longer still. All those he had seen were moving, moving wildly: The little men on the boats were being tossed in waves, and the Venus was turning on her back toward the angel with the mirror, and the girl at her music lesson had leaned forward on the table and was looking over her shoulder at her tutor, and the two figures he had seen today were rocking together while the infant satyrs clambered around them, moving wildly around them.

He shook his head. "Please," he whispered to himself—but it was just to himself. He turned over the card, as if that would make this waking nightmare go away, and then he remembered what else he had thought in the gallery: B . . . B . . . Botticelli. But in his mind's eye, instead of the images of the painting, he saw a figure of a monkey, raising and lowering its hand.

"Mr. B," he said aloud.

And now *he* was clambering. Off the bed, wrapping himself in his robe, out the door, and running down the stairs, his hand along the railing as if it were the lance in the Mars and Venus painting, and he were one of the satyrs. It wasn't so—he couldn't be one of them.

As he entered the kitchen, he thought of going back up, running up the stairs and finding the painting of the farm, and talking to it, trying to calm it down, trying to calm the horse. But it was too late. He was already outside her door; he was already tapping.

He was crying when Madeline opened it; he was openly sobbing, rubbing his knuckles into his eyes like a little child. She took a minute, looking at him, which he could see through the blur from the tears. For a moment she looked like the blue woman.

"Oh, mon enfant," she whispered, forgiving him, forgiving his hasty cruel words before the young man at the gallery. *"Mon pauvre enfant."* She took him then, against her breast, and let him put his head against her and cry and cry, until all the world stilled, as if he were just a baby boy with an innocent face, and the possibility of horns sprouting on his head and fur growing and thickening on his legs could not exist.

~

"Mr. Roskins."

"Master Richard."

"Thank you for the book," he said, handing it across to his tutor. "And for letting me look at it, thank you."

"You're done with painting?"

"Almost."

"Then we can resume where we left off. Do you have your text?"

"Before that . . . well, I was wondering. Remember, when we studied, when you taught me Ovid?"

"Of course."

"There was a myth I was thinking of. The woman who turned into the tree."

"Daphne."

"Yes. How did it go exactly?"

Roskins glanced at his pocket watch. "You do know, I am so fond of Ovid," he said. Then he smiled, and his eyes took on a faraway look and the twitching stopped. "Apollo loved her, but she wanted no part of him nor any husband, god or man. So he chased her, where she fled in the woodland hiding places.

"She was, you see, like Diana, but she was mortal, without power. And when Apollo was upon her, when he had all but caught her, she prayed to be spared, her body to be changed, and then . . . well, the poet says it better than I. She becomes a tree."

"She becomes all still," said the boy.

"Excuse me?"

"Still," he repeated.

"Well, of course." Roskins seemed slightly irritated. "If she's a tree . . ."

"Isn't there another myth?" said the boy. "A myth about Diana."

"Actaeon," said Roskins. "Actaeon the hunter, who comes upon the goddess Diana, surprising her in her bath."

"He watches her," said the boy.

"He *sees* her," said Roskins. "And to punish him, she turns him into a beast—a deer. Horns form on his head, and he is hunted down and killed, torn apart by his own dogs."

"Actaeon," said the boy. "Thank you. I shall read it." Then he looked up at Roskins's eye, twitching once again, and said: "I was wondering something else. I asked once about you, but not about me. Before you were my tutor, I was in school. I was frightened then, that's what I remember. But I never asked you, what you knew, what you understood—why didn't I stay?"

Roskins looked off, through the windows—a few brown leaves were falling—and then to the doorway. "I handle difficult boys," said Roskins. "Boys who have trouble—with others. They said you—you couldn't keep still. They said you couldn't keep your hands to yourself. I don't know if it's true or not. They said, sometimes, something would seem to come over you, and you would try to fight other boys, in a particular way."

"I don't remember that," said the boy.

"It's what they told me," said Roskins.

"What way was it, they said I would fight other boys?"

"They said you were . . ." Roskins looked away, incongruously smiled. "Frantic. They said you fought as if your life depended on it. That you couldn't stop."

~

He felt in a kind of fever now, and when he slept, he almost constantly dreamed. He was surrounded by enemies, and he had to get out somehow. He dreamed of his arms being pinioned, held, and let go, only to become restrained again. His enemies were boys, but they changed into Uccello-like knights, and other times into beasts—satyrs or apes. And the little horse from the painting screamed in his ears. Then all the action would stop, and he would see the man he'd seen at the Corporal's Arms, walking in his funny way, pulling something, pulling a little boat, and his mother was following him, walking behind like in a procession, and the waves had grown still, and his mother was weeping.

Then the boy would wake and think about the house he was living in, and how he'd never asked Roskins, he'd never asked his mother, where he was before he came here, as if he hadn't ever wanted to know. Nine years ago they had come here.

He would sit up, and turn up the lantern, and look at his card and all the *S*'s there, and wonder who would steal the paintings—the gallery owners said they weren't worth much, second-rate copies, out-of-fashion copies with whimsical differences, so then who, other than the boy himself, would want them back?

And then his heart would pound as if it were breaking

through his chest—and he'd think of the story his mother had told him, every scene of it appearing in his mind. Before she'd been rescued, they'd been on a ship, on a pleasure cruise, on a lovely white ship. And there had been a man painting on deck—a man with a walrus mustache—and a beautiful woman dressed as a sailor. And the captain had a little monkey that had scampered all around. They'd sailed across the sea, past the magical islands, and the farms that were there, the harbors with the little boats, the goats and sheep in the fields. And then the storm had come, that terrible storm.

What was the ship called? he'd asked.

It was called *The Diana*.

Exhausted from the effort of thinking, he'd lie back on his bed and try to sleep again. He might dream, and see her face again: at least the face of the blue woman, at least her face staring from a mirror. That an angel was holding. And once he woke with his heart pounding, for the woman whose face was in the mirror was the same as the woman on the swing, and he and the angel weren't the only ones watching. His mother was somehow there as well, his mother—years younger, and she was watching the ravishing woman as well . . .

During the day, he sat looking out the window, thinking about the paintings. He tried to put them together into a kind of fable in his mind: There had been a peaceful farm. And a girl had been all alone, maybe in one of the rooms there, looking in her mirror. Then she had come down for her lesson, and been interrupted at her music. Then she had lain together in a field with a man, and the little boys had seen her. Then she had gone away on the ship. And it was all the same girl, with the same face. No, they were different girls, they were scenes from the lives of different girls. A farm girl, and a girl playing music, and a girl who looked in her mirror, and a girl who had lain with a man. And a girl who had gone away on a ship.

That wasn't the story either.

He looked out the window, at the wide lawn, the fence beyond, leaves drifting downward as if through liquid. Autumn was full upon them, and he thought of how much more of the world he knew now—the galleries, and the museum, and the streets leading back and forth, and the teams of horses pulling the omnibus.

But of course those were things he should know.

He was almost thirteen.

When Madeline came by, she smiled at him and paused a moment on her way to the kitchen. She tousled his hair, and then moved on. Soon she would be eating, zigzag eating, in that American way. After she had comforted him that night, they had sat up awhile, talking. There was nothing he could tell her about what had made him cry, but after some time, she had cried too. And he had been able to understand, in her French and halting English, that when she was little, her father had left them to go to America; after he had gone—it was silly, it was *très fou*—but she and her mother used to eat in that American style. They'd seen it in some etiquette book.

Everyone had their own secret gallery, he thought. Even if he still couldn't make out all the pictures in his.

~

His mother had finally finished writing her personal responses to her readers. It had been some tremendous effort; she had been at it constantly—even through meals, either bringing a letter and inkstand and pen into the dining room, or having Madeline bring in a plate of food to her—please—and then Madeline taking it away later, untouched.

When his mother finished the letters, she carried them from her room in a great bundle tied with ribbon. She smiled at the boy and said she was going to take them to the post. And then she would be stopping for tea. The boy mustn't worry while she was gone.

It was after he saw her walk down the gravel path in the morning light—the bundle of letters bouncing in a sack—that he went into her room and opened her closet door.

There were new clippings on top of the others in the little box—not neatly cut-out stories, just ripped out fragments from a police log:

> *Battersea section: Assistance was offered and declined by the officer on rounds to a man transporting his sick child on a makeshift stretcher.*
>
> *Battersea section: Despite repeated requests from a Mrs. A Foster, the Police Department is unable to deploy the manpower necessary to investigate and apprehend those responsible for the theft of several inconsequential paintings from 10 Hodge Lane and 15 Montrose Walk.*

He peered into the pocket on the jewelry box cover. It was an empty black mouth now, for the bill that had been there was gone as if digested.

As he brought out the painting of the farm, he could hear a ruckus among them—they must be thinking the earth was quaking, that some tidal wave had hit the coastline. He felt glad to see them again, but melancholy too—perhaps for the shaking he had given them, and for what he was going to do.

He's not crying, that's a good thing, said the woman from the window. She was speaking of the horse.

But we can't tell, said the stable hand, *if it's because he's not scared anymore, or because . . .*

Because what? asked Richard.

Because he's even more frightened than before.

He ran his fingers over their surfaces, felt the slight bumpy quality to the paint, as he imagined one might feel with sawdust or the stubble of a man's beard. This painting did not seem to have a classical reference. Of course, it must be a copy too, a reproduction of the one that had replaced it in the dining room. How his mother had both of them was beyond his understanding. Nor did he know why so soon after it had been sold, it had been bought by her nine years ago.

He shook his head, as if trying to clear his thoughts.

I'm sorry for what I have to do, said Richard.

What is that? asked the burly boy. *Martin, Martin, I told you from the beginning, he's a mover, I told you—*

Quiet now, said Martin. *We don't know what he has in mind.*

But I have to. I have to.

Richard looked down at them. He looked over the grass, ran his eyes over the fence, over the river. He could imagine all of it quailing again, as when it had mistaken him for the Creator, who was the painter F Jones: How they had loved to hear his name, how they had burst into pleadings for his mercy.

And before that, when he had wanted to stay: How he had imagined he walked among them, how he had even imagined they could speak . . .

He was even imagining that now.

Martin, he said. *Martin.*

But they were still now, just figures in paint, maybe that way for good. They were figures and he was a mover; and he'd been wrong, it wasn't just a museum within him, but a circus, a carnival, a flowing river. A field dappled with shifting sun, with waving grass. And what else? What else?

He spoke to them one more time as he lifted them from the floor, and held them in his arms, cradling the painting in his arms. The way the light was coming in, he could not only see the burly boy and the stable man, Martin and the horse and the woman, but he could see the two painted-over figures—the ones that looked like drawings done by a child. As if they'd come to the surface to join the others.

I have to do what I'm going to do, he said. *And you couldn't just stay in this room, in this closet in my mother's room. Dark, on your side like that. No matter what the horse saw there before. No matter how scared you are now. There's light out there, there's . . . people. Shops. Museums.* He smiled. *Others like you.*

And just for a moment, he thought he heard them speak again, just that one last time.

We know, said Martin. *We've known all along.*

After a moment, the burly boy said, *There's danger too.*

Chapter 18

He left that same morning, just before noon. He carried the painting under his arm, wrapped in paper and string. He was careful with it as he walked or waited for an omnibus, as he held it in his lap or carried it against his body to pass between the oncoming walkers. So many of them had interesting faces—ruddy or pale skin, facial hair on those of the older men, smooth flesh on the boys and girls, paint on the women.

He kept looking around him as he walked, thinking how he'd have to find this way again, but at night.

It may have been his looking around that did it, for he bumped into a man who unexpectedly exited a shop right before him, who stepped into the street while calling back through the open doorway, "Next time then, Pete." He inadvertently swatted him with the painting, and the man apologized and Richard did as well, and the fellow said, "Well, no harm done, young man." But he worried for a moment that a chip might have been taken out from the canvas, another hole made in the field or river.

It wasn't too much longer that he felt the familiar stones under his feet and saw the narrow drive before him.

Hodge Lane.

He waited for a while in the street, until he got a glimpse

of Madeline. She seemed involved in something new. He could see between the pedestrians, between the carriages passing by, that she was sitting on the floor near the back, by a large sheet of white paper. And it appeared there was something that was dangling beneath her outstretched hands, some sort of automaton—or perhaps a dressed-up pet—that was dancing on the paper. Her mother was speaking to someone who looked like a customer, and pointing out this or that in the two paintings they stood before.

After a moment more he crossed the street, turned the knob—which seemed stiff to his touch—and saw Madeline and her mother look over at him as the little bell tinkled. Madeline got quickly to her feet—she started to run, but evidently thought better of it, and then slowed to a fast walk.

"Have you found it?" she asked breathlessly as she approached, staring at his bundle.

"What?"

"Our painting, the—what was it—*Swinging Woman*?"

"It's another one," he said. He could see she was disappointed. "But it's also by F Jones," he added, which brightened her.

"My mum's cabled my uncle about him."

"About F Jones?"

"I think."

"Why ever for?"

"I'm not supposed to say," she said. She drew away and started walking toward the back of the store. "She's gotten a new lock on the door," she said. He turned and saw a bright black metal catch. He followed her, carrying the packet. She sat on the floor and picked up the figure he had seen: It was a doll, dressed like a little horseback rider. Then she tossed a stone and made the doll jump forward onto the paper. He saw that she'd drawn there a small hopscotch outline: It was as if she had tired of pretending she ran the gallery, and was just being a little girl again.

"Mother won't let me really do this in here," she said. "But I don't always like to be out. So Dolly's playing."

He watched for a moment; it was transfixing to see the movements of the doll as Madeline manipulated her—making her jump on the numbers, her feet together and apart, trying to get to the goal. He watched for a moment. He thought if his mother were here, she would explain to him the origin of the game, how they came up with the numbers, what it meant to throw away the stone and retrieve it again . . . He shook his head as if he were chasing something off.

"What I have isn't your painting, but it might be a way to get your painting back," said the boy, nodding toward the package in his hands.

"How?" asked Madeline. The doll was lifeless again where she held it.

"I'm not sure. But someone took it, and she—or he, or whoever it is—wanted it, and wanted others too. They like the work of F Jones, you see. They really like it. And that's started something—people are looking for it all over the city."

"I know," she whispered. "That's what my mum cabled

my uncle," she whispered. "He's *sought after*. And Mummy told me this: The *F* isn't for his first name, it's part of his last. It's one of those names that have a dash in it. That's a secret too," she said.

"It's a good one," he said.

She turned quickly to the doll—she made it skip ahead, up to the little stone where she'd thrown it. It was leaning over to pick it up.

"If you stop that, I'll tell you something even your mother doesn't know," he said.

She paused and looked up at him, just as her mother began to approach.

"It'll be a secret between us," he said. The doll was collapsed against her hands. "The people who are looking for these paintings . . ."

She was listening to him, tilting her head.

"They might especially want this one."

It had taken a little while to persuade her. The whole time he was talking, Madeline's mother was looking from him to the painting with its paper all torn and lying around it, as if its clothes were in disarray. It must have helped that the customer had left without making a purchase. The lines around Madeline's mother's mouth seemed deeper, and her eyes, when she stared at the painting, had a penetrating gaze. His offer was quite simple: She could have the painting for under ten pounds. While it was no rarity, he did know that the paintings of the relatively unknown painter and copyist F Jones were relatively hard to come by, while being more in demand. She gave him a significant look when he said that, and he imagined her chatting with the young man at Ferguson's, before he and Madeline had gone there that day, and then her leaving the note as a reminder. Maybe after that she'd cabled her brother. She wasn't just Madeline's sweet mother; she knew a good thing when she saw it. For it was like Roskins had said: Things became rare; things became lost and then—strangely—desired. There was no logic to it. He repeated that she could have the farm painting for the price he'd quoted; his French and English aunt wouldn't mind.

His eyes wandered away from her then—his eyes clambered: all around the gallery, over the paintings of the horses and the tree, up around the top of the room, to the second-floor windows, latched and with latches broken.

It was done, then; she would have it. She could look in his innocent face and see that his offer was true, his hair hiding the little horns, his pants hiding his furry legs, his smile hiding his fear of where this might stop.

She just needed to agree to his one additional request: that for several nights it be displayed in the gallery's front window.

Please.

~

Back to his mother's house. She hadn't returned yet, and he just wandered idly around, kneeling on a couch and looking out the window, moving chairs this way and that, going from room to room as if he were once again confined.

Madeline was in the kitchen; a pot of something was simmering on the stove, and she was sitting by the table and gazing at every furnishing in the room, saying, *"le table,* table, *la cheminée,* chimney," as if she were beholding every object and seeing it doubled and changed. He peered at her through the crack in the door, without her seeing. Sometimes she would say a word and purse her lips, not remembering its English equivalent; sometimes she would rub some perspiration from her forehead and neck. Watching without being seen, he felt he was either practicing for what he would do later, or refining a former skill that had fallen out of use.

When he walked in and laid down the sum of money she had lent him, her mouth went into a little O.

~

While he waited for his mother's return he lay on the bed fully dressed, his jacket hanging behind the door. He stared at the ceiling, or paced back and forth, dresser to bed, bed to desk. He took the little sailor doll and as Madeline had manipulated hers on the hopscotch paper, he made it climb up, up along the window frame. When it got to the top, he made it raise its arm, and lower it.

When he heard his mother return, he tensed. She was walking heavily around downstairs; there was an unfamiliar noise—something had dropped or fallen over. He heard her muttering as she must have kneeled to pick it up. She climbed the stairs, slowly. She paused on the landing outside his room, as if thinking over whether to knock on his door, whether to speak to him or not.

Her footsteps resumed as she continued down the hall.

Her own door opened. He was sitting on the side of the bed, waiting for her door to close, for her to grow silent, in sleep.

But her door didn't close, even as he cracked his. He heard her shoes striding across the wooden floor of her room; he heard the covers pulled back. He had never realized how close you were to someone else in a house: It was like Japanese houses with walls of paper—you could almost see through them. He listened for her to unbutton, undress. What he heard instead was another door opening, and then her voice, crying out, thick and slightly slurred. "Oh, you didn't . . . You took it too, didn't you? You found it out and you took that from me too." A silence, and then a steelier tone in her voice, as it lowered, as if she were speaking to someone within the room. "Lord knows why I kept it at all."

She didn't know he was awake; she wasn't speaking to him.

He put his face to his window and saw dim light in the courtyard below, and then two darker places that were moving. It was two men—no, a man and his shadow, walking away from the house through the garden. Stopping. When the man started moving again, Richard saw it was with an odd, rolling gait.

But he didn't think it was this man she was speaking to either.

As the man disappeared, there were other sounds in her room he couldn't fathom—squeaking or whimpering—and then a dull sound like that of a body falling on a bed. And silence.

She must have fallen asleep.

Now he retraced her steps. Slowly, down the stairs. Moonlight coming in through the windows made it seem everything was covered with a liquid film of white. The couches, the chairs, the four places set at the table were all covered with milk. There was even more of it on the side table outside the drawing room—a frozen cascade of white, as if a bottle of it had shattered there. It was the envelopes, spilling from her sack. She hadn't taken them to the post office after all.

He walked to the door and listened, and then looked out, into the night. The man must have gone. The yard around the house was an empty lake of cream.

He went into the drawing room, and took the letter opener in his hand. It gleamed in the moonlight. Back at the table, he picked up a letter, hesitated, and then ran the letter opener along its glue line, the slight ripping sound seeming terrifically loud in the still house, over the barren stroking of a clock. In the dim light, he read:

> *Dear Miss Abigail Foster:*
>
> *I am inquiring about a fine point. It seems that my husband, Charles, and I are in dispute about the proper amount of tip that should be given to the coachman on the nights when he has to wait for my husband outside his club.*
>
> *Sincerely,*
> *Mrs. Reginald Richards*

His mother had scrawled on the bottom what he knew to be an overly blunt, uncharacteristic response:

What is your husband up to in his club?

He cut into another.

Dear Mrs. Foster:

We are most in need of your advice regarding a delicate family matter. Every Christmastide, we are invited over to my maiden sister's house for midday dinner, and even though the goose is always a wee bit stringy we always faithfully attend. Now we would like to have her at our house this year, and want to extend the invitation, but don't want her to think it's because we don't want to be eating her food at her house. You can see this is a most delicate matter, and a quick reply—as it is already autumn—would be most pleasing.

This time, his mother had written several scribbled lines, as if about another matter entirely:

The bond between host and guest—like that between husband and wife—is a sacred one, and so your caution in giving offense is well taken. However, the situation between three of you is most rife with difficulties, and should be broken off immediately, for that is the only way that things can remain smooth and not roiled.

He opened one more.

My husband insists, even in dinner with our relatives, in using his fingers to push his food on his fork. He also uses his knife to eat peas.

His mother's response, marked with blots and cross-outs:

> *Not many realize it, but table manners—like so many of the polite rituals we take for granted—were created to prevent the outbreak of violence, and in this case, at meals. Why is it, do you think, that knives are to be set with their sharp edges facing the plate, that they are not to be pointed at one's fellows or even at one's mouth at table, that they should never be held in one's fist or in any kind of grip reminiscent of a sword or dagger, that Richelieu in the seventeenth century rounded off the points of table knives, if not to discourage assassinations*

Here it broke off.

The form of her writing seemed from a different, desperate hand, and her responses were baffling to him. He had no time to read more, but he wondered, looking at the cascade of letters, if all of her answers revolved around some theme he couldn't quite glimpse. Like pictures on the walls of a room, but the scene in the middle was missing. He had opened them along the glue lines, and when he went to try to lick them shut, he saw more clearly in the dim light the return address she'd put on the flaps:

21 Stanton Lane

Different than 20 Church Walk, the street and number where they lived. But it was the name she'd written above it in a jagged line, her full name as it once must have been, that made everything seem to shift around him, and that through some trick of his eye he only saw now:

Abigail Foster-Jones

Chapter 19

It was strange being out at night, walking rapidly through the streets, feeling the weight of the letter opener in his pocket. He remembered carriage rides with his mother, and looking at figures as they were illuminated within windows. Now he hardly glanced in the shop windows; he kept his eyes searching for street signs, and once more he marveled how one name led to another and if only you paid attention in this sequential way, you could find where you were going or from where you had come.

He saw a couple standing together, embracing, in the glow of a gas lamp, their shadows drawn out behind them; he saw what must be a watchman sitting like a carved man in the doorway of a building.

With everything so still around him, with the moon shadows of every fence post and iron gate drawn on the ground, he had to remind himself he was out in the streets of the city, and not imagining he was in some painting. It chilled him, even frightened him, to think he wasn't, and that there would be no artificial interruption to what might lie ahead. Sometimes through a square of white window, he might see a clock or globe like a blurred face.

Oh, hello. You've come back . . .

But he hadn't. He shook his head. He hadn't.

He walked down the streets he had come to know, and

noticed their differences in the change of light. He saw some men leaving a pub, and stayed well behind them, hidden in shadow, until they walked on, one losing his footing, another singing a snatch of song.

He was getting nearer now. As if he had no dimension, he was not aware of any sensation within him.

He walked on, quickly crossed a road, crossed another one. He hurried ahead, stumbling once on an uneven patch of brick. As if that motion disturbed things, as if he'd made the frame around him tremble, he saw before him a movement.

Down the narrow street, in the milky light. He halted, froze. He was an etched figure again. Then he took two steps, and knelt behind a gate.

He could see the figure moving. The figures. Down the narrow street, and now turning. Turning down Hodge Lane.

But they kept walking past the gallery, without looking left or right, and he slumped to the ground.

After a moment he looked again; there was no one on the street.

He just lay there as minutes ticked by. Like some figure of wood, he was powerless to move on his own, and had to wait for this outside animator.

Somewhere a clock tolled two. Somewhere a cat cried, someone stumbled, cursed. He was lying there with the cold brick against his cheek, the brick that was gradually staining, growing the slightest bit darker from his tears.

He heard a sound of footsteps, scampering, from the other side of the lane. He looked down the blurry street, sideways in his sight. Saw two moving figures strolling up the lane, one with a roll of something. He wouldn't even get up as they walked past the gallery window of 10 Hodge Lane.

They were almost out of sight when they turned and walked back.

A string jerked him up. The figures were slowing by the gallery window. He wiped his eyes: His vision had never been clearer. It was a man with a child. His head lowered, seeing it was a man and not a woman, not the blue woman, come to take her paintings back.

The blue woman, whoever she was.

He didn't want to think who she was.

It was the likes of no child he'd ever seen; it was walking with its feet and hands, arms as long as its legs, walking with the man past the gallery window of 10 Hodge Lane, one more time turning and walking back.

The man was wearing a hat. He was tall.

They stopped before the window. The man lit a match and held it forward; the flame doubled in the window glass. Details of the man's face suddenly appeared, a portrait miraculously painted and restored. Deep-set eyes, sticking-out teeth, mustache—walrus mustache.

The man shook out the match and his image dissolved. In watching that motion, in recalling his face, the boy had lost sight of the little figure. Where had the little figure gone? He saw another movement up alongside the building, the color of the figure blending into the discolored brick, only its movement making it visible as it climbed the wall.

Mr. B.

He was back there for a moment, as before him the monkey raised its arm and reached for the top of the second-floor window. He was back in his memory, in the room with the three of them in a row, reflected in the mirror: the tall man painting and he pretending to paint and the monkey raising its arm in imitation. And she laughing, and his little boy's voice saying, "Mr. B's funny."

You're funny too, she'd said. And she knelt and kissed him.

B. B, said the man. His teeth were sticking out. *Can you say it? Can you say Botticelli?*

Of course he can't. He's only a little boy.

The tall man had trained it to get his brushes, to take the canvas from the easel and lean it against the wall.

She hates it, she hates it, says it's not civilized, the man said. *Damn her, but I'll have him painting someday.*

Oh, now now now, she said. *Now now now now. Na na na naaaa.* Her sweet voice, the door closing, and the boy was outside. And somehow there was the angel with the mirror, holding it up to a woman's face.

Standing now on the street, he closed his eyes a moment and pictured his mother's face: If you took away years, if you dressed her in blue, if you undid the ribbons below her chin . . .

That wasn't the story either.

He opened his eyes. The monkey had reached the latches; it opened the window. It was inside. Something else the man had trained it to do, said he never had to worry about anyone locking him out.

The monkey swung from the windows in its little blue sailor suit. It disappeared into the blackness of the gallery, maybe using the paintings as footholds, maybe rubbing its furry legs across the renderings of ladies, the gentleman with the collar and tie. It took a little time before the door rattled—maybe it had tilted its head at the other paintings, trying to make sense of what it saw.

From inside, the knob turned and the front door opened without a sound. The man walked quickly inside past the new lock, and removed from the front window the painting of the farm, where Madeline's mother had agreed to place it. There was a flicker of white: Still inside the gallery the man was wrapping the painting in paper, covering over the fields and the river, the burly boy and Martin and the horse. The horse would be scared.

Moments later the man emerged, closing the door behind him, joining the beast, again looking like a man with a child as they proceeded up the street.

The boy had watched all of this as if it were quite unreal, and it took him a moment to register what had happened, and to realize that unless he acted quickly—unless he himself moved—they would soon be out of sight.

If they had been more than a couple of blocks ahead, he would have lost them or been seen. They walked rapidly, and he had to skip from shadows of garbage bins to shadows of houses, shadows of outbuildings to those of carriages, moving and then going still, while before him the man sauntered with the wrapped painting and the rolled-up something beneath his arm and the monkey ran quickly and then slowly, hopping up on low porches and then back down to the street.

The man stopped abruptly. He seemed to listen for a

moment. Richard heard it too, the whistling, the low voices of people approaching. Richard squinted ahead, up the street, and when he looked at the man again, he saw that the configuration was changing. The tube beneath his arm was being unrolled to form a rectangle of cloth, and the picture laid beneath. The monkey was clambering up onto what had become a small litter in the man's opened arms, and burying its head and body in a sheet.

"I say, now, everything all right?" said one of the men who had been approaching.

"Is your little chap all right? Big lad, isn't he?" said his companion.

"Just taken with a fever," said the man with the walrus mustache. A deep, grating voice. "Not too close now, let's not disturb him. Just taking him to the doctor's."

"Good luck, then."

"Good night."

As the two men continued on their way, the supposed child clambered down and scampered ahead as the man rolled the stretcher back into a tube, and once more placed the painting beneath his other arm.

They turned down a street; the sign for it angled strangely up above Richard when he passed it moments later. *Stanton Lane,* it read, white letters on a blue background—the street of the return address she'd put on her envelopes. But it had never been *her* address. He was back again in his memory: It was daylight. He was walking down the lane with his arm lifted—his hand in someone else's. The chimp was running this way and that, and she was smiling. It was she who had his hand, and she was gorgeous. The light was playing over her face, and she was saying, *He'll be here, he'll be here soon, see he's left us his nice pet.* And the boy thought of the man being there and how the door would close, and in the glorious light of the street like in an Annunciation she said, *Don't frown, my little man, don't frown, see you've made Mr. B frown too, you've made Botticelli frown.*

He had to remember it was night now, on a cold brick street; it was years later. He had to remember to stay in the shadows, watching the figures ahead, the little one now walking the same way as the man, like a tiny double.

Of course he recognized the house. To think of it being here, so close to Hodge Lane, not more than fifteen minutes away if you walked quickly. 21 Stanton Lane. Three stories, brick. It looked abandoned now, derelict. They had lived on the first floor, Richard and the blue woman, although for a moment he didn't know if he had been called Richard then.

But why is it called the first? he'd asked them once.

He's awfully bright, said the man. *Too bright for three. The way he looks at me. What do you see in that little mind of yours?*

He's just three. Go ahead, tell him.

The tall man leaned over and spoke through his mustache, and Richard remembered how the hair blew away from his mouth and his teeth were sticking out. Sticking out. The words were not unkind. *The first is the ground, the second is the first.*

He laughed then, saying in his wee child's voice, *The second is the first.*

And she laughed too.

He remembered bouncing up the stairs on the man's shoulders and having to duck his head, and both of them laughing, and to him it seemed the steps were stories below.

And then later, when the boy was alone with her. With her. With her.

His hair is gray and his 'stache— said the boy.

Mustache. Mus-tache.

His mustache is brown.

You've already got a good color sense.

Color . . . ?

Seeing the way things are.

The memory left and it was night again. Years later. And yet looking at the house, he felt he could find it anytime—sleepwalking, surfacing from a nightmare. He watched as the man opened the unlocked door and swung the package through. The chimp had scrambled ahead.

He stood there in the dark. The street seemed so much smaller than he'd remembered, the other houses shorter, some boarded up. They had used to look like forts or castles.

A dragon lives in that one, she had said once, *and a witch in that.*

That's not where the witch lives, said the man.

Come now, not in front of him. What about when he has to visit her?

We'll just say children should be seen but not heard. Especially at Sunday luncheon. She'll like that.

Hush now.

She will.

Light came on in the first floor. The first floor that was

really the second. Its soft glow spread, and the boy wondered if somehow, miraculously, she was still there. If the scenes in his memory and the scene before him had somehow joined together, separate lines meeting in the vanishing point. Then the man would have brought the painting back for her; he would have simply brought it back for her. Once again she'd point to the woman in the window and—

We'll call him the burly boy and him we'll call Erin, she'd said to the boy.

He pointed to the third.

We'll call him—Martin, she said in her lilting voice. *Martin. I'll tell you a secret.*

Yes?

Your father's name was Martin.

He's not my father.

No. Your father . . . I hardly knew your father. But he's ever so nice, Mr. Foster-Jones, ever so nice, don't you think?

No.

Come now, say he is.

He is. He's not.

Come now.

He is.

Good. And this one we'll just call the horse. He's a good little horse.

He is? Why? Why is he good?

He's happy and he likes everybody. And he's never afraid. Not even when he has to be alone.

Oh.

Not even then.

Oh.

Hush now.

He remembered where the painting had hung. In the room it had hung.

Maybe the man was hanging it there now, this scene he had painted. All these years later, but the same moment in time. Time didn't pass in that room. He was hanging it and she was pointing the figures out to him, and telling the boy their names . . .

He had to stop a moment, his eyes welling.

If it were the same room, and she were somehow there again, then he could run up the stairs and find her. *Hello—so nice to see you again!* He would say it and she would say it at the same time, the way they used to.

He began to move, in a way he couldn't remember moving before, and he wasn't sure where it would stop. Fast, but careful. Flowing across the street, up the steps; turning the handle and then in through the door. A flight of stairs ahead of him. He climbed them swiftly, silently, two at a time. Climbed like a little monkey, a little beast.

Don't call him that, she'd said to Mr. Foster-Jones.

All right, all right. I just meant he has such a way of getting into—

You want him to like you, don't you?

I don't really care. Now, stop it, he said to the boy. *Stop looking at me that way. I hate how he looks at me.*

Don't you—

All right, all right.

Richard climbed the stairs. The door was open on the upstairs landing. He wondered where the chimp was—if it saw him it would scream or bare its teeth. The chimp had never liked him. It wouldn't do to be found out like that. He had to see them first, without them seeing him.

The way he once had.

It was coming back to him now, more of it was coming back. Here was the landing and the door and yes, of course, the picture that was there, opposite the door. He could see it now, ahead of him, in the dim moonlight, on the left wall. It was hung there again; stolen, and hung there again. Of course he'd never seen it in a museum; he'd never been to a museum, never been to the Netherlands. Never been a gypsy boy a-roaming. He walked slowly toward it and looked up.

An angel holding a mirror.

Hello—so nice to see you again. It's been so long, not really any time at all.

There was something odd about the picture, something about the Venus's face, about R Venus's face, reflected in the mirror. He couldn't see clearly enough in the brown light to tell.

He turned. There was the door. Paint peeling: That was different. What was the same was that it was closed again. Closed again, with the two of them behind it, and him out in the hall.

He stood there a moment, and as if the string that had been holding him was cut, he fell to the floor.

He didn't hear any sounds, any footsteps. If they had heard him, she would be coming out now, she would pick him up. He would lean his head into her and sob. And she would say, *Oh oh ohhhhh. La la laaaaaa.*

The burning in his eyes made him sit up. His heart pounding in his chest made him sit up. So much was working inside of him.

He remembered now, what he used to do. When he was out here, here in this hall, with the angel and the woman with her face in the mirror. He'd curl his fingers, a little wave good-bye to her. Then he'd leave her, and she would never move. He'd leave her for that other door, and when he came back she would still be there, and she would not have moved.

The other door, the second door, to the other little room, also on the right. What was there—that they didn't know about? That took a boy with sharp eyes to see at all? That took a little monkey to get into?

He stood in the hallway, still, his heart racing, picking up all his stymied motion. He reached out for the wall to hold himself steady.

You used to do that. When you looked up at us, said the angel.

Yes.

You were so little then.

He drew his hand quickly away, as if it had been burned.

The other door—he had found it near the end. But why did he think that word *end*. There must be a history to that word—an origin, a linkage. A lineage. Or perhaps it had always meant the completion of something, the finish, the closing of a circle. He only knew he dreaded to enter, and yet he forced himself to walk slowly past the closed door that was the door to the bedroom and then to the second closed door.

He reached for it. He opened it.

A rushing in his ears.

It smelled of dust. There was nothing in it now. There used to be some kind of squat piece of furniture. He used to look at it, and climb up on it, and jump down from it, and think it was a table that had eaten too much for supper. It was a fat table. And when he'd played ships, it was a ship. It was an island. And he was the captain on the island. He was the captain spying.

He turned around in a slow circle. There was something he used to do, when he had started playing at ships. Something in this room, across from the rocky island. Inside the other door that was there, inside the closet. All her dresses had been hanging there.

He opened it now. Empty. He moved his hand through the empty space, as though he could still hear her dresses rustle, still hear the wooden music of the hangers. Still smell the fabric of her dresses, some of them salty like the sea.

He lowered himself to the floor. To the floor of the closet. He had done it the first time just to be among her dresses, to feel them draping him as he knelt there—so much better than being alone in the hall.

It was too dark in the closet, and he felt with his hands. He felt the crack where the floor met the wall. He felt where the crack was interrupted by a piece of wood. It wasn't the real back of the closet here; just a piece of wood placed on the spot where the plaster was thinning, where the holes had been punched through.

Punched through by a little hand.

Three small holes, two on top and one below. The two on the top were like binoculars. He had played at ships and then he'd made the binoculars, punching through the thinning wall when the room was empty. He'd become a captain, a sailing captain, looking through binoculars.

She had told him his father had binoculars. She knew that about him. He had binoculars for looking at the seabirds.

For looking out on the calm, calm sea.

He closed his eyes and held still, before he pulled the wood away. He waited a moment. He hung his head.

He brought his eyes to the holes.

He hated to do it, but he had to. He had to look out on the calm, calm sea.

Sorry. Not polite at all.

He saw a map of a coastline, framed. And on the next wall were all the paintings he'd been tracking. In two rows, on one wall. He could see them in the light that was somehow moving. The paintings were hanging there once again: the little men going out to sea in their boats, and the girl interrupted at her music, and the man and the woman lying in the field with the little goat-men around them, and the painting of the farm, and the blue woman on the swing, with the blurry face like in water.

He stared at them, one by one. They were there together again, as they had once been. Once. She would have wanted them together again. Looking at them now, he could see why.

The faces of the women in the paintings were different than those he had seen in the museum, in the books.

He knew now what he never could have known then, why F Jones had made the duplicates, how they were reproductions with a difference and what the difference was: the blue woman in the swing, and the girl interrupted, and the Venus with Mars. He could see her on one of the little boats, and could look up at her in the angel's mirror.

The man had painted them all with her face.

They did, after all, tell a story.

His eyes blurred to see her, and he had to bring his head away while he silently wept.

He could hear a voice now. The man's voice. As he listened and looked again at the pictures, he could imagine they were the ones speaking: a little man on a boat, a satyr with a shield, and the music tutor behind the surprised face of the girl interrupted.

Aren't you glad to be back?

Aren't you glad to have them all back?

Just like it was.

I've brought you all back.

The man he couldn't see was speaking to someone out of sight of the binoculars he was viewing through. It would be she, it would be *she* the man was speaking to. He could see the green rug, and the light that was moving over it in a most unusual way, like slanted rays across an ocean. But he couldn't see where the man was, and what was moving the light. He couldn't see *her*. He felt frightened then, and angry, just as he once had, that the man was speaking to her, that F Jones was speaking to her and the boy couldn't see. And that she didn't run out of the room for him.

The voice of the man halted. And in the sudden silence the boy's gaze held on the paintings; he stared into the compassionate eyes of the paintings.

Do you want us to take him away? asked the little men on the boats.

He could be with her—like that, said one of the goat-boys. *And it would be he, it would be his face on the warrior in the grass. On the Mars in the grass.*

She would be with him in the grass, said the Venus.

And she wouldn't want to be interrupted, said the girl interrupted at her music lesson, the man standing behind her. *She wouldn't want that.*

Would you like us to take him away? asked the little men on the boats.

Would you like us to take her away?

You could just paint her over, said the burly boy.

What's he saying, what's he saying, Martin? asked the stable hand.

He wouldn't say such a thing as that, said the woman whose face was a smear.

We can easily take her away . . .

No, not that, never never that.

And the blue woman on the swing just said, *Na na naaaa, ta ta taaa, oh oh oh.*

He remembered now, the slow dance he had seen them do. How it had gotten quick and then slow again. On the sea he looked out on. On the deck of the ship. On the rocking white ship and the sheets shifting like foamy waves across the wide expanse of her bed.

The man had said, *I'll always come here. Always, always. Say, always.*

Oh, always. Oh.

Then the man was painting her as she sat so still in the room, and one time the boy was there, looking on, raising and lowering his hand like the man. Twitching his hand to make hair, like the man did. Dropping his hand to the pretend paints at his side. One time the man was gone, and after her bath as she looked in the mirror, she let the boy paint her face.

Lipstick, she said.

Lipstick.

Rouge.

Rouge.

See, that's where he kisses me.

Kisses you.

You're a good painter too.

And then he came back, F Jones came back, and he roared, the walrus roared, the sea howled and the boy was swept out. He was out in the hall and he was crying and the door was shut hard. But the boy knew then, knew he could go to the holes in the wall. Knew he could look through the spyglass in the wall.

One time they had danced. They had danced, they had danced, they had danced. And the monkey scampered around from one painting to the next, while they danced. Mr. B was visiting the islands of the farm and the field and the place for the little boats. And the white ship rocked.

One time they had danced, and she had said . . .

What had she said?

She said, I can't anymore, said the Venus in the field.

She said, You can't keep coming here, said the girl interrupted.

She said, I could still be your model. A girl has to live. With a boy to raise. And I always liked being your model. But not here, not anymore, said the woman with the smeared face.

The faces in the paintings looked to the boy and said, *Now aren't you happy?*

And he looked back at them and said, *Yes, you understand.*

She said to the man, *Because I can't anymore. I can't bear to see her. To sit at the table at your house with the two of you, and she going on about your eating.*

He said, *She'd never expect.*

But I know, I know.

Then we can go away. We can go away somewhere. We can sail away, said the man.

No. You can't keep coming here, she said.

I have to. I have to. I will.

And then she said, *Yes, there's someone else. He doesn't have a wife who's—he doesn't have a wife at all. He's very young, nice. He's French. You might like him, under other circumstances. No, he doesn't paint, he's not an artist at all.*

You won't like that, a satyr had said to the boy.

Like what? he had asked, walking through her room. She was out somewhere. It was an afternoon, and light was pouring in. It was glorious. He was walking through her room, looking at her face in every pose.

Another one, said the satyr. *Another one she'll dance with, another one where you'll be outside the door. Outside with just her face in the mirror.*

You'll want him to go away, on the ships.

Do you want us to take her away on the ship?

And the little horse had cried and cried.

He had come again, F Jones. Mr. Foster-Jones had come again. He wasn't supposed to, but he had come again. She had locked the door to him, but he got in. Mr. B had gotten him in, gotten him past the threshold. The boy had seen the animal come in through the second-floor window, the second-floor window they called the first, where the latches were open; the beast had pushed against the glass and it had opened. He was trailing his hands on the floor, heading back for the top of the stairway, and the boy had screamed. The chimp bounded down the stairs, unlocked the door below. He let the man in the door. Footsteps pounded up the stairs—the man found her in her room. Kicked open her door and found her in her room. And the bond between guest and host had been shattered.

I've brought you a new one, he said. *Look at it!* Her face was in his hands, and the boy was running around. *Look at it! It's a surprise.*

You shouldn't be here. You get out of here.

Look at it.

I don't want to—

You've got to look. Now her face was looking—he had made her look. And the boy was crying. The boy was running at the man, he was beating his fists against the man, and the man hardly noticed.

I did it for you. Look, look at it. She's surprised in her bath, don't you see?

No, take it away. Take it away. He shouldn't see that. He's of an age. Don't you touch him. But he shouldn't. See that, or see this. She was crying, and the boy was crying. *He's of an age. He shouldn't see his mother like that.*

Don't you see? the man said. *It's Diana,* he said. *Diana, surprised at her bath.*

And then the boy was out in the hall, and the door was closed. He was out in the hall, and he was lying on the floor and he was hurt and he was crying and then he was beating his hands on the door.

But he didn't know how you could watch, said the angel in the mirror.

No, he didn't know that.

From the next room you could watch.

Yes, I—

You saw her pull the painting from him, and throw it down. And turn to the others.

She turned to us, said the tutor in the music lesson.

The man couldn't believe what she was doing. He couldn't move at first.

She tore us all down, said the girl interrupted.

Like a storm she tore us down, said the little men in the boats.

We fell in a fury to the ground, said Erin.

And he couldn't stand to see that, said the satyr with the lance.

She said, *I don't want them anymore.*

She said, *He'll see them, he'll get jealous.*

She said, *Don't you dare touch me.*

But he did, said the boy.

Yes, don't you remember? Then the man finally moved, and they were moving in the room, they were moving, moving quickly, he and she, back and forth. She was saying and then he was saying, and his voice ahhhhh and her voice ahhhhh and her voice no. His hands around her face, holding her beautiful head in his hands, and her head was moving and his hands were moving and then they were still. He took his hands away from her. She fell to the floor. To be with us. He put his face in his hands. We were looking up at him, from the floor, all of us. We could see he was crying, and he looked at us—and her face was everywhere in us. Looking up at him. Still, looking up at him. In the paintings, still, and her own face, still. For now she was one of us.

The man walked in a circle. He said, What have I done? He said no. He said now he had to call her. She had to come, he had to call his wife to come. To see what he'd done. To see what she'd made him do. To see who she'd married, and what he'd done. And let whatever was going to happen be done.

She came, said Martin, not looking at the boy. *His wife came. She was crying and he was crying and her sister's face was everywhere looking up at the two of them crying. Her lovely face, her still face, that looked almost like her older sister's face, beautiful and composed and still.*

You were crying, said the Venus in the field to the boy. *You were peeing and crying in that little closet, and she said, The boy—have you even thought about the boy? I always cared—I always felt bad for the boy. She found you and the door opened behind her and the light poured in and she took you in her arms. And when she hugged you, you thought she was your mother; everything was blurry and she was dressed in blue and you called her your mother and she said yes, she said na na naaa, she said la la laaaa, she said yes.*

He had his hands over his ears, his eyes were shut.

No, the rest, they said.

He could still hear it.

The rest.

He could still see it.

She covered her over, said the girl interrupted. *Under the waves of the sheets her sister covered her over, knelt down and covered her over. The sheet billowed up and then down and she was gone, billowed up and then down and she was gone. The world was gone.*

She held you in her arms when the other man came, said Martin. *When the other man came and pulled her away in the sheet.*

I remember the little boat of the sheet.

And still her face was everywhere in us, you saw her everywhere you looked.

I saw her everywhere . . . I still see her everywhere . . .

And the monkey was standing there . . .

I still see him everywhere.

. . . all that time, raising and lowering its hand . . .

He momentarily blacked out, and he woke up choking, not understanding where he was. Not remembering, and then all at once knowing everything, knowing it all. He started choking again, and spitting up. Curled on the floor of her closet. Nine years later.

When he looked up, he saw the dim light filtering through the holes in the wall. They didn't look like binoculars anymore, but an open mouth and two slit eyes. The face of a satyr. And the light behind it was once again moving, and it made the satyr's eyes shift and roll. The man's voice was once again speaking softly.

He was speaking to someone in the room.

Richard spit up again. F Jones was the Creator—and had he brought them all back? The paintings. And the boy. And her as well . . .

Had he somehow brought them all back?

He heard the words now, his mother's words, in F Jones's gravelly voice. *La la laaa. Na na naaaa.*

The boy strained to see into the room; he put his face to the eyes of the beast, he looked through them. The light was moving, and he could see in the light the eyes of the paintings, as they had looked at him, such a little boy. The compassionate eyes, the forgiving eyes of the paintings . . .

He brought his face away. It was years later. He wasn't such a little boy anymore. Slowly, he moved backward from where he was kneeling. He felt in his pocket for the letter opener, what he'd used to slice through *21 Stanton Lane,* through the name *Foster-Jones*. He crawled out from the closet and stood in the darkened room. For another moment he was overcome by crying. He thought of his mother—no, it would be her sister.

It would be his aunt.

Now we'll take our tea. We'll pour the milk in. We'll butter the bread. See, you're taking tea like a big boy. Look, you can eat all that bread.

The poor broken women. The poor poor woman. And the poor broken boy.

Two for the queen.

Three for the king.

Beggar your neighbor!

He thought of the one who had beggared them.

Weeping, he walked down the hall, past the angel, past her face looking shattered in the mirror.

She had said, *I don't want to.*

And he had said, *Look.*

I don't want to.

You've got to look.

His cloven feet echoed on the wood. His heart was pounding as he touched the door, as he gripped the silver opener. He remembered now, beating boys, flailing past them, his fists going into them, unable to stop. Into them, into them. If he rushed the man now, if he thrust his hand forward, he would never stop. If she was somehow there, he would save her this time. Or do the same to her, it suddenly didn't matter. There was nothing else to do, there was nothing else that mattered. He pushed open the door—he stepped over the threshold, as he'd been waiting his whole life to do. He saw Martin and the stable hand and the burly boy, and the horse.

The horse began its terrified screaming.

The horse had seen movers, and he was one now. He was

one. He strode forward, his legs thick with hair, the horn wrenched from his head ready in his hand. He was trembling, trembling all over, standing there breathing hard as the shadow of the door glided past and the other part of the room became visible to him. He heard footsteps running, pounding up the stairs behind him, as in the dim, moving light he saw the scene before him.

She was propped on the bed. In the white sheets. It was she, it was her face. There was no question. And he was making her up, this man Richard must have thought of his whole life. Lipstick. Rouge. He was an old man now, and he was speaking softly to her, gentle syllables coming from his mouth, his gray mustache blowing out over his teeth as he made her up. *Rouge. La la laaa. Blush. Ta ta taaa.*

The boy looked at her through his slit eyes; he tilted his head. It took him a moment to comprehend that her face was a face in a painting. And that the makeup was paint: The man was painting her. Fashioning her there, out of thin air—remaking the last painting he had given her. The chimp was standing in the corner of the room, holding a lantern in its hand. Raising it, and letting it fall. Raising it, and letting it fall. It made the shadows shift; it picked up first this color and then that in the paint on the canvas, all the undertones in the canvas—as if the woman there were blushing, or turning pale, or just slightly moving her head. This woman undressed, with the look of shock on her face, the water dripping from her, the man in shadows afraid. It was Diana—surprised in her bath. And she was beautiful—he'd made her so beautiful.

And Actaeon had seen her and been turned into a beast and it would tear him apart till he died.

The footsteps were pounding up the stairs; they paused, went this way, then that. They thudded in the room behind the boy, and at the moment of their arrival the boy moved forward, with the letter opener outstretched, and the horse screaming in his ears as behind him he heard Abigail's voice: "No!"

F Jones turned, while the painting stayed still. Richard stopped and tilted his head—the man alive, the woman in the painting not. He took another quick step, kicking through years of propriety. But killing him wouldn't bring her back, and something in all those years was slowing him. Stopping him. For the longest time it seemed he just stood there, shaking, as she came up behind him and F Jones—quite surprised at the interruption, and wholly mad—turned back to the painting of his mother's face. The boy lowered his head as the silver letter opener dropped from his hand.

He'd stopped himself, he hadn't rushed the man.

The horse had stopped screaming.

After a moment he looked to the woman behind him. To the woman in the painting, and the woman behind him. Then he ran past her down the stairs.

She found him, pacing back and forth, choking on the street, back and forth from the shadows to the light of the streetlamps. She came up and put her hand on him—"Now, now, now . . ." until finally he stilled.

"There's so much," she said. "'Sorry' wouldn't—" She

shook her head and started weeping. "He's been two months out of hospital. I didn't think I could bear it."

And the boy was shaking and sobbing, tears staining the bricks beneath his feet.

There was suddenly another man on the street, standing in the shadow of one of the houses. He approached through the light and the darkness and said to her, "I've told you he's here. I've told you I'd come with you." He glanced at the boy, and then away. "I even clued you about the boy, finding his way here." Through the noise in his ears the boy recognized the voice of the tramp who had come to their house.

She reached into the pocket of her coat, and handed him a folded bill.

He didn't move for a moment. "All right," he said. Then the man turned and, in his shiny boots, he walked toward the house, through the darkness and light, where the man in the room was still painting.

TRICK OF THE EYE

Chapter 20

For months he hadn't felt well; it took that long for it all to settle down in his mind. He let himself think about it once again as he looked from the window of the train on which they were traveling.

"That man," he asked her. "The tramp. Why was he there?"

"He was someone who knew about these kinds of things," she said. "That kind of life. Long ago he'd been a friend of your father's."

"My father," he said. He felt very little. His father, he'd learned, had been a seaman on leave, had met his mother one week and left her the next, pregnant with him.

"I'd hoped the police would discover it as a series of thefts by a madman, a matter to be quickly disposed of. When that failed, I had to call on that man again. And he came and fetched . . . my husband . . . back to the hospital," she said.

"Call on him—again?" said Richard.

"Nine years ago, he was the one who made the arrangements—for her." She faltered again. "For the—" She broke off.

"He took her away on the ship," said Richard.

"There never was any ship," she said.

They had left the city proper; the lawns were larger here,

the houses farther back from the road. Carried upon the rhythmic clicking, they were passing woods and fields, the outbuildings of farms. Looking past her profile where she sat next to him in the compartment, he could see a parallel road through the opposite windows of the train, where carriages were moving.

His mother's name had been Annabel. Her younger, more beautiful sister, Annabel. It tolled in his mind like a chime.

For two months after it had happened, when he was just three, he hadn't spoken. Then in his little boy's voice, hoarse from disuse, he had told Abigail about a terrifying dream he'd had, a nightmare about a ship going down. It wasn't long after that when she had come up with the story of the ship. His mother and father had been on board; and yes, it was terrible when the storm came. But she'd survived—and she would be coming home, coming home soon. Night after night she had told it, until in his young child's way he had opened his arms to her, and once again called her *Mum* and *Mother* and *Ma,* and she had finally said *yes, yes, la la laa.* Closing her eyes, her tears moistening his neck, she told him, *Yes, I've come back.* And it became a story of a ship sailing past magical islands, and aboard there was just some woman who looked a little like her, some woman dressed in blue, growing smaller in the rising waves.

She hadn't wanted a scandal, especially considering its effect on her profession. Her profession was all she had left. So she'd helped her husband leave by railway, to the north, promising never, never to return. In the north he had broken down, and been confined to a bedlam hospital. She quietly moved from their lodgings, relocated to another section of the city—a widow with her young son, her sweet child, who only sometimes woke up screaming.

She hadn't wanted a trace of her husband around, this man who had taken pity on her sister and her young son, who gave her money for rent and food, and took her on as a sometime model—until his feelings swept them all away. She sold all of his paintings to galleries, as she needed whatever money they would fetch. But something about the scene of the farm haunted her, and two weeks after she'd sold it, she bought it back. Perhaps because they'd once talked about moving to a farm, where she could have a field of roses, and he could paint all day in the plein air. Or perhaps because it seemed more alive than the original, and the artistry of his hand in it reminded her of something good in him. Her sister's face was nowhere portrayed within its placid fields.

Outside the frame of the train window, a goat dropped its head to feed on the grass; someone in coveralls was sliding open a barn door.

Richard remembered the day he had stopped hating them all. The day he was no longer so filled with his terrible wishes. He was picturing the portraits the man had done of his mother. He had almost spoken it aloud, almost turned to her and said it—forgetting it was her husband he was speaking of. But the thought burned through his mind.

He had meant to love her.

All the entrancing poses of her face could, after all, tell a story.

He had gotten up and stood by her, so quietly, she didn't notice him at first, as she kept on with her reading. His mother's sister. His mother. He had gazed out the window of their house, over the lawn, and beyond. To a little boy it would all seem a sea, a vast surface where just your tiny ball of a head was floating. And she had stopped for him, put out the rope. She had taken him in, devoted herself to him over the years. Beneath the formality of their interactions, there had always been this powerful current. *That* was the force that finally slowed him, that stopped him in his last headlong rush.

In her manner she loved him.

Madeline had moved on. She had managed to save up enough for her fare to America. She would do anything to find her father. Sometimes at night when he couldn't sleep, he would envision her holding out the map for him; or practicing his language; or comforting him, forgiving him, saying *"Mon pauvre enfant,"* until all the world stilled.

They left the train at a country station. Before hiring a carriage, they had a simple meal on a heavy plate in a small noisy room. Abigail seemed easier with her manners; he ate quickly, and went outside while she finished. A wind had come up, ruffling the grass, rippling the flag at the top of the station. He walked around to the back, through smells of sweat and leather, past horses drinking from a trough; he stood near as a stable hand backed them into the traces of carriages, and fitted them again with their harnesses and blinders.

She didn't mind, and the driver seemed as glad for the company, so Richard rode the final leg on top. Some of those coming toward them—horsemen or other carriage drivers—seemed to know their man, and they waved at him, to be answered by a wave in return. Sometimes they'd clap their hands on their heads to secure their hats, but still the brims would ruffle, and their locks of hair would wave.

"It's blowing in right for March," said the driver.

Richard could see the school before they even reached its drive. It too was surrounded by fields, but it was smaller than that which he had gone to when he was younger. Or maybe it was just that he was older now. It was of gray stone, and there were doors spread along its front, and windows going up four stories, to a flat roof. Chimneys with smoke—and the smoke was blowing, tumbling away. There were boys running, others walking, some pausing to watch. And he too was also capable of such things—of movement and of the ability not to move.

For one last time, he thought of the paintings. Not only the ones in that room, but the others. The knights in the Uccello, and the couples in the Watteau, and the saints and the virgins and the angels. Shipwrecks and deserts, horses and dancers, and all the guises of her ravishing face.

Good-bye. Good-bye. They were arrayed before him in their magnificent poses, splendid in their light, and still and perfect in their illusion.

Good-bye . . .

The carriage was speeding up the drive, the horses were pounding, and he saw all at once that the doors and windows before him were so many frames, openings into colors and shapes, landscapes and figures. But these were openings into other worlds. Of all those he would meet. Worlds of shade and light. Of love. That he could go into.

Good-bye.

That he could really move into.

The Paintings

In order of appearance in the novel, here are the real paintings Richard encounters, and where they can be found today:

St. George and the Dragon. Uccello. c. 1455–1460. National Gallery, London.

Skittles Players Outside an Inn. Jan Steen. 1652. National Gallery, London.

Peasant Wedding. Pieter Bruegel, the Elder. c. 1568. Kunsthistorisches Museum, Vienna.

Battle of San Romano (one of a cycle of three paintings). Uccello. c. 1435. National Gallery, London.

The Conversion of St. Hubert. Master of the Life of the Virgin. c. 1480–1485. National Gallery, London.

Disappointed Love. Francis Danby. 1821. Victoria and Albert Museum, London.

The Rokeby Venus. Diego Velázquez. c. 1649–1651. National Gallery, London.

Girl Interrupted at Her Music. Johannes Vermeer. c. 1660. The Frick Museum, New York.

Dordrecth: Sunrise. Aelbert Cuyp. c. 1650. The Frick Museum, New York.

Mars and Venus. Botticelli. c. 1480. National Gallery, London.

Diana and Actaeon. Titian. c. 1559. National Gallery of Scotland, Edinburgh.